"Lauren, we've got to get out of here,"
Colt said.

"We have to call the police," she said, staring at the man on the floor. "He stabbed Mav. We have to help Mav." She was numb, completely numb, and knew that shock was moving in on her. Shock that she'd shot someone. That she'd taken a man's life. It made little difference that he'd been planning to take hers first.

"Who's Mav?" Colt asked.

"My dog. He . . . he saved my life."

"There isn't time."

"What do you mean, there isn't time?" Her words sounded slow and thick.

There were probably very few things that could have snapped her out of her shock at that moment. But what happened next did.

The dead man opened his eyes.

Dear Reader,

It's spooky, the way our Shadows novels just keep getting eerier, more romantic—and *better*—all the time. Take this month's offerings, for example.

First up, new star Evelyn Vaughn returns to "The Circle" in *Burning Times*. This sequel to her immensely popular first book, *Waiting for the Wolf Moon,* features Brie and Steven Peabody. But Steven is not quite himself these days, and if Brie can't figure out what's wrong and then return him to himself... Passion and possession make a heady mix in this story that, once begun, will prove impossible to put down.

Our second book this month is also *this* author's second book. Allie Harrison made her debut as part of our "New for November" promotion. Now she's back, and in *Dead Reckoning* she's outdone herself in the sexy scare department. Once you're dead, you're dead, right? Maybe not—as Lauren Baker learns when a series of "accidents" begins to threaten her life. Only one man could be behind them, and only one man— Colt Norbrook—could save her. But would even Colt be a match for an evil from beyond the grave?

But the not-for-the-faint-of-heart fun doesn't stop there, because we'll be bringing you two new Shadows novels every month. Don't miss them!

Yours,

Leslie J. Wainger
Senior Editor and Editorial Coordinator

Please address questions and book requests to:
Silhouette Reader Service
U.S.: 3010 Walden Ave., P.O. Box 1325, Buffalo, NY 14269
Canadian: P.O. Box 609, Fort Erie, Ont. L2A 5X3

ALLIE HARRISON

Published by Silhouette Books
America's Publisher of Contemporary Romance

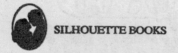 SILHOUETTE BOOKS

ISBN 0-373-27040-2

DEAD RECKONING

Copyright © 1994 by Allison Harris

This edition published by arrangement with Harlequin Enterprises B. V.

® and TM are trademarks of Harlequin Enterprises B. V., used under
license. Trademarks indicated with ® are registered in the United States
Patent and Trademark Office, the Canadian Trade Marks Office and in
other countries.

Printed in U.S.A.

Books by Allie Harrison

Silhouette Shadows

Dream a Deadly Dream #20
Dead Reckoning #40

ALLIE HARRISON

has been writing since she was in school but never really took it seriously until she joined her local RWA chapter three years ago. She now works to divide her time between her husband, their two small children, reading the latest hot romance and creating her own intriguing stories.

She lives in a small town in Southern Illinois and believes everyone should follow their dream and never give up.

As always, to Wayne, Ben and Rachel
with love

And to Jenny, for the name

PROLOGUE

"I'm telling you, someone is trying to kill me."

Lauren Baker let out a breath, doing her best to hide her feelings and not let the sound resemble an angry, frustrated huff. She continued to look at Colt Norbrook, who was sitting behind his desk. His eyes were darker than night, and despite the bored expression on his face, those eyes never left hers. Well, she thought, at least he was still listening to her. She laced her fingers together on her lap, knowing that if and when he grew bored with the conversation she'd have no choice but to pick up the ashtray on the corner of his desk and sling it in his direction.

"If someone is trying to kill you," he said evenly, "why come to me? You should be taking this up with the police." His voice was so calm, it was almost seductive.

Lauren bit her lower lip. It was a bad habit, she knew, but right then it was either bite her lip or bite his head off. "I did take this to the police, but there wasn't any real evidence that someone was trying to actually kill me." She fought to hold his gaze. It wasn't that she felt ashamed at not being able to convince the police. It had taken her long enough to convince herself. It just wasn't easy to return the hard look in those black eyes.

His brows rose slightly, revealing for the first time a loss of control over his emotions. "So why do you think I'll find any evidence?"

Lauren pressed her hands tighter together. She really wanted to hurl the ashtray at him. "I'd hoped you'd have more sense. Besides, it's what you do, isn't it?"

"I would think anyone who gets through the police academy would have to have some sense," he replied, not answering her question, his voice taking on that seductive tone once again. But the grin he gave her shot that seductive air straight into orbit. She watched his mouth for a long moment, then had to shake away the thought of how his lips would taste.

"I can see I'm making a mistake, Mr. Norbrook." She stood, shifting the large envelope she held so that it didn't slip from her hand.

"Wait," he said, stopping her. "I never said I didn't believe you. Why don't you just show me what you have."

Lauren hesitated for a moment, looking once again into those dark, depthless eyes, wondering if there was any hope of his believing her. She wondered, too, if he'd stopped her merely because he saw some look of desperation on her face that she hadn't been able to mask. Then she returned to her seat. Slowly she opened the envelope. "All I have are newspaper clippings," she said, without looking up at him. "The police refused to let me see any reports or anything."

"Are you saying that these incidents were all labeled as accidents?" he questioned. His eyes left hers, and he looked down at the newspaper articles she'd placed on his desk.

"I don't know for sure," she replied. "I do know that the incident at the bank was no accident, and that it was investigated fully. And even with the description of the robber I gave the police, which was confirmed by the tellers and other people in the bank, as well, he still has never been caught. There were several articles about it in the newspaper. And besides, it was a robbery. It wasn't like a chandelier fell on my head or something.''

Was she mistaken or were his eyes twinkling? She looked for another moment before glancing down at the clippings on his desk.

''And the other incidents?''

''I never found any indication they were investigated, so I think they were labeled accidental, but I'm not sure.'' She looked at him, watching him for any more signs that he didn't believe her.

The room was quiet for a long moment as he studied the clippings. ''Tell me about the bank incident,'' he muttered, looking at the newspaper article.

''Well, I was in the bank in Rock Hill. I own the Rock Inn, just off Route 17, on the lake, and I went to make a deposit.''

''How much?''

''What?'' she stammered.

''How much money were you depositing?''

She blinked at him, her anger returning. ''Mr. Norbrook, I don't see where that's any of your business,'' she snapped.

He ignored her snappish tone. ''If you were carrying a great deal of money, and someone found out about it, it could be why you became a target.''

Lauren shook her head slightly. ''It was only a thirty-dollar deposit, money for me to hold a room for a client for the Memorial Day weekend. Besides, I'd already given it to the cashier when the man with the gun came into the bank,'' she explained.

He looked up at her, and she saw that his dark eyes weren't really sparkling. What was in them looked more like dark fire. "It says here he didn't get away with any money."

"Exactly," said Lauren, nodding. "The cashier took on this really clumsy attitude. I guess she was stalling for time, or maybe she was really nervous. Either way, she dropped a great big stack of bills all over the floor before she could hand them to him. And it just makes me wonder why he didn't shoot her instead of me."

His gaze met hers, his look hard, the twinkle or fire or whatever it was gone in an instant. "You're the innocent bystander who was shot?"

"Yes. The bullet passed right through my arm. It hurt a lot, but it healed rather well, and quickly," she added, hoping he didn't dwell on the subject. The thought of having a gun pointed at her still gave her nightmares.

"Is anyone staying at your place now?" he asked softly.

Lauren looked at him for a long moment, until his gaze met hers. She was totally caught in the dark ocean of his eyes, and a wave of warmth touched her. She swallowed, trying to ignore it.

"No," she nearly stammered, her voice tight. "I don't take any reservations from the middle of April through Memorial Day so that I can spring-clean and get the house into shape for the summer season."

"Can you tell me what this man looked like?" he asked. He suddenly seemed much more interested than before.

"I can do better than that. I can show you." She leaned over the desk, drawing closer to him. The clean scent of his after-shave touched her, sending a tingle up her spine that she tried to ignore. "See here?" she said, pointing to one of the news articles. "A picture of the scene of the school-bus accident. That's him right there." She pointed. "And here he is again in the picture of the scene of the hotel fire." She pointed to another picture.

He stopped, stiffened visibly. "You're sure that's him?"

"Yes. That's the man who tried to rob the bank. Believe me, I'll never forget his face." Her gaze held his, and she wondered just what he was seeing that caused him to tense.

"Where were you when these were taken?" he asked quietly, without looking up at her.

She watched him. "I only stayed at the bus accident long enough to give my statement to the police. At the hotel fire, the police and firemen wanted everyone out of the way as soon as possible. As soon as they saw I wasn't injured, I was ushered to another hotel."

He was finally looking at her. "So you never saw him in person?"

"No, only in the pictures."

"Have you ever seen him before?" His gaze held hers.

"No. I never saw him before the bank robbery."

"You don't remember seeing him at the scenes of the other accidents?"

"No."

"Is this all?" he asked, his fingers sweeping the clippings aside.

Lauren shook her head. "There've been other things, and they seem to be increasing in number, and happening more often." She had his attention now. She nearly smiled, thinking that if he didn't actually believe her, he was at least listening to her. Which was more than the police had done when she called them last week about the heavy breather on the telephone.

"Like what?" The question was harsh.

She shrugged, not really knowing where to begin. "There was a gas leak at the inn. The brakes failed on my truck. I've been having problems with the telephone. Either it's dead or someone calls, then just breathes." She could have gone on, but she didn't.

"And the police didn't believe you after all this?"

"Well . . ." she began. "They didn't exactly not believe me. They took everything down in a report and watched the house for a week. But when they saw nothing going on and no one around but me, they said there was nothing they could do."

"Did you show them these and tell them this is the guy who robbed the bank?" His question came out harsh, as though his throat had grown tight.

"Yes," she confirmed. "And they said they were still looking for him. But until they find him, he's stalking me."

"Do you have any idea why this guy would want to kill you?" His voice was tense again. If she hadn't known better, she'd have thought he knew this man in some way.

"No."

"None?" he asked, pressing her. "Are you sure?"

"Yes," she replied, just as forcefully.

Colt was first to tear his gaze away. "I'll tell you what," he said finally. "I can't make any promises but I'll see what I can find out about this man."

"Thank you." At the moment, it was all she could ask for.

"Can I keep these for a few days?" he asked, indicating the clippings.

Lauren smiled for the first time since entering the office. "Of course."

Nearly fifteen minutes later, Colt Norbrook looked out his window, down three stories to the street, where he watched Lauren Baker climb into a pickup truck. They'd met before, of course. He'd crashed his cart into hers in the grocery store. But he'd never guessed she'd be his first client. He'd never expected her to come waltzing into his newly organized office and ask for his help.

What a beauty, he thought. All that red hair had seemed to be calling out to him to touch it. He'd thought the same thing when he crashed into her in the store. He shook his head, thinking what a mistake he was surely making by even taking this case long enough to check out the guy in the picture. But the fact remained, the man in the picture bothered him. He hadn't seen that face in six months, except in his nightmares. What bothered him even more was the fact that one picture had been taken in Kentucky nearly two months ago, and the other only three weeks ago, here in Rock Hill. And even Colt could see that it was the same man in both pictures.

Yes, that man bothered him. Almost as much as Lauren Baker intrigued him—and frightened him. He knew she could be dangerous, as dangerous as the maniac in the pictures, only in other ways. She could destroy everything he'd worked to become in the past six months. Still, that didn't stop him from wanting her. And that was why he'd promised to find out what he could.

He continued to watch out the window until she drove away. Then he turned back to the pictures that were still spread out on his desk and looked down at the man who was trying to kill Lauren. A shiver of rage mixed with cold terror passed through him. He didn't want to face this man again. He wasn't sure he could face him again and live through it.

One thing he was sure of, however—he had to do everything he could to keep another innocent victim from falling into the hands of this maniac. He had to. It was as simple as that. Colt was the only person who could stop him. He was the only person who really knew who the man in the picture was, the only person who understood just how far this man in the picture would go. And he had no choice but to make sure that Lauren Baker wasn't this man's next innocent victim.

Colt stared at the picture. A shiver of coldness passed through him again. He could have sworn the man's gaze in the photo had shifted—to look up at him. Letting out a deep, ragged breath, Colt turned his thoughts back to Lauren Baker. Desperately he tried to fill his mind with thoughts of her, in an attempt to erase the icy terror that plagued him.

God help him.

God help them both.

CHAPTER ONE

Thunder echoed in the distance. Lauren stopped her planting to listen, absently wiping away perspiration from her temple. She'd wanted to get the bulbs planted before the rain started.

As she looked out over Red Lake, her thoughts turned to Colt Norbrook. Again. Hardly five minutes ever went by without her thinking of him. His dark eyes still haunted her, and his dark hair and looks had been so compelling she'd had to work to keep herself from conjuring up his face in her mind. She knew he'd just started his practice as a private investigator here, and she had the feeling she was his first client. But he was the only P.I. in Rock Hill, and she hadn't wanted to travel all the way to Springfield to find someone else.

More than once she'd had to stop herself from phoning him to see if he'd found anything in the past four days. Surely he would have called if he had. Unless, of course, he thought her story was a joke. If that was true, she figured, she might just strangle him for raising some hope in her. Twice today the breather had called.

She told herself over and over that she only wanted to contact Colt because of the caller. It had nothing to do with the rich sound of the private investigator's voice. Nothing.

The sound of breaking glass in the kitchen brought Lauren's head up in a snap, Colt Norbrook and her planting forgotten instantly. A tremor of cold fear moved up her spine, and despite the warm spring day, she shivered. The house was open, and Lauren looked up at the screen door. It took her only a moment to realize that everything around her had grown still. There were no birds or insects chirping. The soft early-May breeze had even ceased blowing.

She looked around. Where was Mav? That dog was always around, always close to her.

"Mav?" Lauren called softly. "Mav, where are you?"

She stood up slowly, the great weight of fear making her ascent difficult. Someone was in her house, her inn. She'd given Merell, the housekeeper, a much-needed vacation until Memorial Day, when the first guests were due to arrive. Her only other hired hand was Pete, the groom, who took care of her horses and did odd jobs around the inn, and she'd seen him leave close to an hour before, his workday finished. Besides, he spent most of his time with the horses. He wouldn't be around the inn.

A sense of being totally alone struck her with the sudden intensity of a bolt of lightning. Even Mav was gone.

She stared at the screen door. But she couldn't see into the kitchen. It was too dark, with the quickly approaching sunset and the oncoming clouds of the approaching storm. Her eyes never leaving that door, she walked slowly toward it. Her stomach churned with terror, and her chest tightened.

This was her home, her inn. She'd worked hard to make it what it was, and she wasn't about to let anything or anyone destroy it. Not without a fight, she thought, trying to swallow down the terror building within her. If she could only control the shaking of her knees.

From inside the house, more glass broke. The sound of it brought her to a halt. The few steps she'd taken had brought the sound so much closer, making it so much louder. It took almost all her energy just to draw in a breath. She forced her legs to move on. Although it couldn't have taken more than a few seconds to reach the back door, it seemed more like hours. Slow, agonizing hours that allowed the sick fear to build in her stomach.

She pressed herself only as close as necessary to the screen in order to see in. The kitchen was empty. She could see no one. There were, however, two broken plates on the floor. Lauren gasped at the sight.

She stood there, rooted to the spot, for the longest time, staring at them. Then she reached out and grasped the handle of the screen door, but she thought better of opening it. Dishes didn't just jump out of cabinets. And whoever had pulled them out could still be in there, hiding, waiting for her.

No, it would be stupid for her to go in there. She let go of the handle and took a step away from the door. She thought of heading for her truck and driving into town, but her keys were in the kitchen, on the table, and she wasn't going in there after them. There was a phone in the stable—she could call the police from there. She took another silent step away—

And bumped into the large, warm form of a man who was standing behind her. She realized with the sudden intensity of cold terror that the plates had been broken only to divert her attention.

Her scream was cut off by the large hand he clamped over her mouth. The shining blade of a knife came around her in his other hand, and she was pulled up against him, her head bumping into the hardness of his chest. Panic and terror washed through her in an instant, bringing with it a wave of dizziness.

"I've waited so long for you to be alone and not behind the safety of a locked door. I'll make it quick, I promise," he whispered into her hair, his voice sounding harsh and raspy. His breath touched her ear and brought a shiver up her back. "It will only hurt for a moment."

She could feel the strength of him radiating through the arms that held her and in the hardness of the rest of his body pressed against her back.

The knife moved closer, toward her face, toward her throat.

Lauren didn't think. There wasn't time. She knew death was near, and she merely reacted. She grabbed the blade of the knife with one hand, ignoring the flash of hot pain that passed up her arm in the same instant. She hit him with her elbow at the same time she stomped on his foot.

He released her with an oath, a sound that was filled with more frustration than pain. And she stumbled away from him, landing hard on her knees on the bricks of the walk. She didn't waste precious time looking back at the man with the knife. She pulled herself to her feet and moved away from him, sweeping away from the brush of his hand as he tried once again to grab her.

He might have caught her had it not been for Mav. The full-grown German shepherd came running from the side of the house, jumping the man from behind. The weight of the dog on the intruder's back was enough to knock him forward, unbalancing him and making him stumble onto the walk.

Lauren didn't think about which way to go. Once she was out of the man's grasp, she simply kept moving. The kitchen door was directly in front of her, and she scampered in, closing and locking it behind her. She looked through the window just in time to see her would-be killer sink his knife into Mav's stomach. The large dog yelped and fell away from him. Lauren screamed, bringing her hands to her face, her scream passing through splayed fingers.

The man turned his attention to her. To her horror, he came toward the door. She pulled the shade and jumped away.

"Open the door, Lauren! You can't hide from me forever!" His raspy voice came through the door, through all the open windows.

My God, she thought, the whole house was open, every single window—with nothing to protect her but their thin screens. She ran to the kitchen window and slammed it shut, leaving a bloody print from her cut hand. She turned the lock just as he pressed his face up against the pane.

"You're wasting your time, Lauren," he said, his words sounding muffled through the glass.

With a gasp, she jumped away, seeing the intruder up close for the first time. Her heart was racing, her knees felt weak and threatened to give out beneath her. He was the man from the bank. The man who'd been photographed at the scenes of the accidents she'd recently experienced. Just the sight of him caused her breath to catch in her throat. For a long moment, she simply stared at him in horror. Seeing him so close, face-to-face, brought back a memory. She'd seen him somewhere before, somewhere other than the pictures and the bank, but she couldn't remember where.

What should she do? Call the police? By the time they got there, she could be dead. By the time she got them on the phone, she could be dead. Her best chance was to get out of the building, to get away from *him*. She knew it was only a matter of time before he got to her, and she didn't have the time to wait for some knight to ride in on a horse and save her. She had only herself.

She grabbed her keys from the table and turned back just in time to see him leave the window, heading around toward the building's front. Lauren raced through the house to the front door. Not that she could do much good—even if the door was locked, he could just take his pick of the windows.

In the living room, beside the large brick fireplace, she grabbed the poker. Thinking of Mav, she felt a sob build in her throat. She fought it down again, knowing she didn't have the time now to think about her dog. She grasped the poker tightly. She wasn't about to make this easy for him. No, she owed Mav that much.

Looking out the window, she saw the man race past. Sweet heavens, he was going to beat her to the front door.

She reached it just as he did, and for a moment she thought she'd be able to get it locked before—

The door crashed open against her, hitting her shoulder and shooting pain down her body, knocking her right off her feet. The poker slipped from her hand when she landed on the hardwood floor, and it fell several feet out of reach. Her keys flew out of her grasp, as well, landing somewhere across the room, out of sight.

She let out a startled, choked cry and looked up at the man towering over her. His broad form filled the door, silhouetted against the quickly clouding sunset.

Lauren's breath was coming out in pants. Never taking her eyes off the man, she tried to slide away, edging along the floor. Warm tears of fear slid down her cheeks, and for the first time, she was feeling the throbbing from the cut in her hand. She tried to ignore the pain, concentrating on moving, mere inches at a time, across the smooth floor.

Then he smiled and it was enough to freeze her heart. He looked as if he was at a picnic.

"Lauren," he said. The simple sound of her name brought enough terror to tighten her throat and make it difficult to draw in a breath. He really meant to kill her.

He wielded forward the knife he still held. It was laced with blood. Her blood. And Mav's. She recognized the knife as one of her own that hung on the board in the kitchen, the one with the tiny nick in the blade, that she always used to peel and slice apples. Her initials had been carved in the handle by one of her past guests.

"No," she murmured. Slowly she shook her head, finding the situation too hard to believe.

"I told you before, I'm making this as painless as I can," he said. "It's useless for you to fight me."

"No," she said again, still sliding away slowly. She would never give up. Never. She had her inn, her guests, her horses. Everything she'd worked so hard to build.

Her hand slipped on the blood from the cut, and she fell onto her elbow. More pain shot through her arm, mixing with the icy terror that had long ago filled the rest of her. She was now at the doorway leading into the hall, and he took a step into the house. "Why?" she whispered. "Why are you doing this?"

"I'll explain it all to you later," he replied, taking a step closer. Then another step, and another. His footsteps were silent on the wood floor. Yet his menacing form seemed to fill the entire room.

His words didn't make much sense, her logical mind cried out. Later she'd be dead and wouldn't need any explanation. "What?" she stammered. If she could keep him talking, maybe buy herself a little time...

He drew close enough to reach down and grasp her foot.

She instantly turned cold at his touch and tried with all her strength to pull away from him. "No, please..."

"It's no use," he said. To her horror, he was still smiling. "You belong to me."

"No!" She struck out at him with her other foot, kicking him several times just below the knee. His smile never faltered, and his grip on her never lessened. He pulled her across the smooth floor toward him.

"You're so close," he said softly. "There's no escape." He raised the knife. "My promise still holds—it will be as quick as possible. Look at me, and it will all be over very soon."

"No." Grasping the doorway, she looked away. She didn't want to see his smile, his anticipation. The fact that he was enjoying this and so looking forward to killing her brought about a whole new wave of terror-filled nausea.

He raised the knife high, with every intention of bringing it down into her. Even though she still refused to look directly at him, she could sense the movement. Involuntarily, she screamed.

A shot rang out, with a deafening sound that echoed through the house. The force of a bullet knocked the man into the doorway just above her. He fell to the floor with a heavy thud, landing just next to Lauren. His face was toward her, and his cheek rested in the small pool of blood that had formed from the cut in her hand.

For a long moment, everything was completely still. Lauren glanced down at the man, but she was still unable to move or breathe. He looked so handsome, so calm, as he lay close to her, his eyes shut.

A shadow fell over her, and she turned her head slowly to look at the man who'd fired that fatal shot. Her eyes met those of Colt Norbrook. He still held his gun, aimed and ready, at the man on the floor. She released a long breath, and felt the throbbing pain in her hand. The pain was almost as strong as the fear tightening her chest.

"He...he was going to kill me," she said softly.

"I know," Colt said, his eyes now focused on the man on the floor. "Dear God, it really is him!" he gasped, awestruck, his voice breathy. "Even looking at him, I still don't believe it."

Lauren began to tremble, her terror finally building out of control. Her breathing sounded loud in the quiet room. Still without looking at her, Colt reached down and grasped her arm, sliding her away from the man with the knife.

"It's him," she panted. "The man from the pictures in the newspapers."

"Get the hell away from him, Lauren," Colt said roughly, still pulling her away from the man on the floor.

When Colt's gaze finally met hers again, she saw that hot, dark fire burned brightly in the heat of his eyes. His look caused heat to wash through her and touch her somewhere deep within. She blinked at him, and thought the feelings must be due to the terror that was still swirling through her. Then he pulled her to him, and with one hand he pressed her against his chest. Lauren leaned against him, feeling weak and slightly dizzy. But the warmth of him helped ease away the icy terror. She rested her head on his shoulder, wanting, needing, only to stay close to him. She could hear his heart racing wildly.

"Why are you here?" she whispered, leaning away just enough to look up at him. Her throat was still so tight with fear that it was hard for her to talk. She wasn't sure why she even asked, she was so glad to see him.

"I was able to dig up some information on that son of a—" He glanced at the man on the floor and let his breath out in a harsh rasp. "And I thought you should know about it. Let me see your hand."

She held up her hand like an obedient child, not caring about the fact that she was staring at Colt Norbrook. Her knight *had* come to save her. When he took her hand in his large one, Lauren couldn't get over the gentleness of his touch. A warm spark passed up her arm, and she found herself wanting to lean against him again.

He swore at the blood and tried to wipe it away with the edge of the shirt he wore. More blood oozed out. He tore the bottom edge off his own shirt and wrapped the cloth around her hand. "It doesn't look that deep, but it is bleeding a lot," he said. "Can you move your fingers?"

Lauren flexed her fingers, trying to ignore the pain, to show him that she could. "Is—is he dead?" she asked in a small voice.

"I sure as hell hope so," he replied, and Lauren was taken back by the venom in his voice.

"It looks like it," Colt added. He let go of Lauren's hand and moved away slightly to reach out hesitantly toward the man on the floor, searching for a pulse.

Just then the man's eyes opened and he looked right at Lauren. Those eyes were filled with such confidence.

She gasped in terror.

The man moved quickly. In a moment, Colt was knocked away from her by the force of the man's fist colliding with his jaw, causing him to crash into a nearby chair before tumbling to the floor in a dazed heap. His gun flew from his hand, landing not too far away.

"I've been waiting to do that for a long time, Norbrook," the man said. His voice was laced with ice, and it sent shivers up Lauren's spine. Then he turned his attention to her.

"You know him?" Lauren whispered, her voice too tight with fear for her to get the words out louder.

He smiled a cold, wicked smile. "Oh, yes. Norbrook and I go back a long way." Then he reached for her.

Lauren screamed and tried to scramble away, moving in the opposite direction this time toward the front door. He grabbed her arm, his fingers biting into her soft flesh. She screamed again, horror so strong in her that she thought she must be choking on it. She tried to pull away from him so hard that her feet went out from under her and she landed once again on the floor. She kicked out at him with all her strength, but he refused to release her arm.

Out of the corner of her eye, she spied Colt's gun resting innocently on the floor. She reached for it, grasping it just as the man holding her slid her closer to him in an attempt to pull her to her feet.

She didn't even remember pulling the trigger. One moment she was close enough to feel his breath on her face. She looked into his eyes, and she saw in them everything she feared. She saw death. She saw his strong intent to kill her.

The next moment, he was propelled away from her, finally releasing her arm as the bullets from the gun entered his body. He crumpled to the floor.

Lauren stood still, staring down at him, the gun still aimed at him. Not that it would do any good, she realized. She'd used all the bullets. The gun was empty.

"Lauren, we've got to get out of here," Colt said, pulling himself to his feet. His jaw and chin were already swollen, but he didn't seem to notice.

"We have to call the police," Lauren said, still staring at the man on the floor. "He stabbed Mav. We have to help Mav." Her voice sounded flat. She was numb, completely numb, and she knew without a doubt that shock was moving in on her. Shock that she'd shot him—that she'd actually taken a man's life. It made little difference that he'd been attempting to take hers.

"Who's Mav?" Colt asked, his voice sounding harsh.

"My dog," she replied. "He..." She couldn't stop the tears from coming to her eyes. "He saved my life."

"There isn't time," Colt said beside her.

"What do you mean, there isn't time? We have to find Mav." Her words sounded slow and thick, even to her. Yes, shock, or something very much like it, was setting in quickly.

There were probably very few things that could have snapped her out of her shock at that moment. But what happened next did.

The man on the floor opened his eyes again.

CHAPTER TWO

Lauren couldn't seem to order her feet to move. It was as though her brain had shut down from fear and could no longer coerce her body into obeying. It was impossible, she thought. There was no way in the world he could still be alive.

The man was looking at her once again, his eyes filled with that same fearless confidence. He pushed himself up, slowly. He reached out and grasped the knife that had fallen from his hand. Then he was on his feet. Slowly he walked toward her. His eyes held hers.

Lauren shivered at what she saw in those eyes. Lust. Hunger. Passion. A passion unlike any she'd ever seen before. It was a passion to kill her.

Lauren blinked at him, unable to believe what she was seeing. There were holes in his shirt where she'd shot him, yet she could not see one drop of blood. She let out a panting breath. "Oh..." she moaned, unaware that the sound she heard was that of her own voice.

Colt's fingers dug into the upper flesh of her arm and pulled her hard enough that she very nearly lost her balance again. "Come on!" he said, his voice sounding raw.

He dragged her out the front door.

"Come on, Lauren!" Colt yelled once more, pulling her down the front steps of the porch and to the drive.

A motorcycle was parked behind her truck. He released her arm only long enough to climb aboard. "Get on!" he ordered.

Lauren looked back at the house. The man with the knife was coming quickly down the front steps toward them.

"Move, Lauren!" Colt yelled again. He started the cycle and revved its engine.

"But what about Mav?" She felt she had to do something. She'd be dead if it wasn't for Mav.

"Forget the dog," he growled at her. "We can't help him."

"I can't just forget about him. He saved my life."

He looked up, and Lauren followed his gaze, seeing the man with the knife growing closer, quickly closing the gap between them.

"All right, where is he?" Colt asked, his voice rising.

Lauren climbed on behind him, instinctively holding on to him, spanning his waist with her arms. "Around the back, near the walk heading down to the dock."

Colt turned the cycle around and headed toward the side of the house. Lauren rode the bumps of the walk, the uneven lawn and the roots of a large oak tree with him. He took the bike right through one of her flower beds. Lauren didn't care.

They reached the back of the house, and Colt stopped. They both looked around. Mav was nowhere in sight.

"Where is he?" Colt asked, revving the engine slightly.

"I don't know." She pointed. "I saw him fall right over there."

"Maybe he went into the woods. We'll call the police as soon as we can so that they can be on the lookout for him."

"Then he isn't dead," she said, her voice filled with hope.

"Look," Colt was pointing now.

Lauren looked up and saw the man with his knife coming around the corner of the house. He was running toward them.

Colt put the bike in gear and took off in the opposite direction, heading toward the other side of the house so that they could make their way around to the front.

Lauren looked back to see the man reach the walk, the same place where he had stabbed Mav.

He spoke to them, and Lauren heard his words clearly even over the revving of the cycle's engine. "It's only a matter of time, Lauren! And your time is running out!"

She dared to meet his gaze. His expression held only a small trace of disappointment. She turned away before his spell took over her again. Pressing her face against Colt's back, she felt relief wash over her, along with his comforting manly scent. Her shock at shooting that man had left her, reality crashing in the instant his eyes had opened. Just thinking about it brought about a fresh wave of fear, causing her entire body to shake. She held on to Colt tighter and closed her eyes.

She breathed deeply, letting his scent calm her. She kept her eyes closed, not caring where he was taking her, as long as it was away from the man with the knife, away from the fear that man had brought her. She just wished she knew where Mav was.

Colt touched her hand, and gentle warmth moved into it. But her other hand, the one that had been cut when she grabbed the blade of that knife, still throbbed painfully. And on top of the physical pain was a continuing feeling of terror, so strong she thought it would never diminish. Fighting the fear and fighting that man had taken all her energy. She was exhausted. At that moment, she wanted nothing more than to rest against Colt Norbrook. She could hear his steady, strong heartbeat, and she concentrated on it, relishing the stability of the sound.

Lauren wasn't sure how long they traveled. It could have been mere minutes. It could have been hours. The only time that held any importance for her was the seconds dividing Colt's heartbeats. When he finally brought the motorcycle to a stop, Lauren was dazed and tired, and her hand was hurting. She welcomed the pain. It was strong enough to push aside her worry over Mav. It wasn't quite strong enough to push aside her fear, but it did give her something else to think about.

She heard Colt's voice, sounding soft and close. "Lauren, let go." He shifted slightly to turn toward her, and his shoulder moved beneath her cheek. His muscle flexed against her skin. Oh, he felt so good. She didn't want to let go. She didn't want to move at all.

"Where are we?" she asked quietly, still refusing to move or let him go.

"The Rock Hill Hospital," he replied, his voice vibrating through him. She could feel it against her cheek. "They can fix up your hand here."

She only tightened her grip on his waist. "No," she said simply.

He shifted, trying to turn to look at her. "What do you mean, no?"

She pressed her face closer against his shirt so that his manly scent filled her and kept the disinfectant smell of the hospital from touching her. "I hate hospitals. I'm not going in there."

"Lauren—"

"I'm not going in there," she said again, her voice rising. "Please take me someplace else, anyplace else. I don't care where."

He hesitated, looking back at the hospital. Then he let out a sigh. "Fine," he muttered, starting the motorcycle again.

They traveled farther on, and Lauren went back to relaxing against him.

She was, however, still holding his waist tightly when he stopped again. The warmth of his hands touched hers again, and this time he pried them loose from his waist. He had to help her climb off the cycle. When she did, she stood on shaking, weak legs that threatened to give out at any moment. With his warmth gone, the spring breeze that touched her brought on a shiver.

Her gaze met his. She wasn't quite sure of everything she saw in his eyes, but she could identify inviting warmth, a pool of comforting darkness she would have loved to fall into.

"How?" she asked, her voice sounding breathless. "That man, how could he just get up after—" She couldn't make herself say the words.

"I don't know. Come on." He took her uninjured hand and propelled her toward the door of a log cabin.

"Where are we?" she asked.

"The other side of the lake."

Lauren went with him without thought. She looked around with only slight interest. "Is this where you live?" she asked.

It was a rustic place, surrounded by trees. Lauren could see the lake beyond the corner of the cabin.

"Yes, when I'm not at my office. I thought about taking you there, but it's on the building's third floor, and it would be an easy place to be trapped in." He didn't look at her, he was too busy glancing around them.

Lauren noticed his guarded expression. "Do you think he followed us?" she asked softly.

He finally met her gaze. "Even if he didn't, it wouldn't be hard to find out my address."

"Then you think he'll come here for me?" she asked flatly, finding it hard to believe it was her life she was discussing.

"Yes. He seemed pretty intent on killing you." He stopped walking for a moment. "Why?"

"I don't know," Lauren replied softly.

He looked at her as though he didn't believe her. "Come on," he said, leading her inside.

She looked around the cabin with a sweeping glance. There was one large room, divided by a stone fireplace in the middle. The fireplace was open on both sides, so the kitchen could be seen through it from the living area. The furniture was simple, but comfortable looking. There was a large bed against the far wall. Besides the back door, there was one other door, which Lauren assumed led to the bathroom.

Colt locked the door behind them. "Sit down," he instructed, moving her toward one of the chairs in the kitchen. "I'll get something to fix up your hand." He left her and went into the bathroom.

Slowly, still dazed, she sank into a chair. She closed her eyes for a long moment, only to force them open once again when the man with the knife filled her vision. She didn't want to think about him. She wished she could somehow forget the entire experience.

She shifted her gaze to the large window in the kitchen door. Darkness was falling quickly, and more clouds were moving in, but she could still see the lake rippling in the breeze. It looked so ordinary, so usual. She wondered how she could feel such fear while everything else around her appeared so unchanged.

Colt returned with a bottle of antiseptic, several balls of cotton and a roll of gauze. He pulled a chair close to her and sat down. Gently, silently, he took her hand.

Lauren liked the feel of his touch. His hands were strong, but not too rough. They sent their warmth right up her arms. She watched him closely. His high cheekbones and strong features gave him such a look of stability, of strength and pride. His dark hair glistened. She fought the urge to reach out with her other hand and touch the tanned skin near the nape of his neck, where she'd only have to flex her fingers to test the softness of his dark hair. Her attention was taken away only when he touched the antiseptic to her hand in an attempt to clean it. "You're Native American, aren't you?" she asked softly, looking back at him.

"Part, yes," he replied softly.

"What kind?" she asked, liking the sound of his voice.

"Cheyenne. My grandfather lives on a reservation in Montana." His eyes met hers suddenly, and Lauren had the feeling that he couldn't quite believe he'd revealed so much to her. Then he touched the antiseptic to her hand again.

"This is going to take a few minutes," he said quietly, as she flinched away from his touch. "Try and relax."

She tried. She really did. But she'd just experienced too much in the past few hours. Fear and pain were surging through her. And his nearness wasn't helping, either. She wanted to lean against him, so that he could hold her and his warmth could fill her entire body, leaving no room for anything else.

He finished cleaning the cut on her hand and shifted, moving slightly away to reach for the gauze. Lauren fought against the desire to grab him and keep him close.

"Don't you think we should call the police?" she asked softly.

He looked up from her hand to meet her eyes. "I'll call and report Mav as soon as I'm finished here."

"What about the...rest?" she asked quietly, not wanting to describe anything else.

"You said the police didn't quite believe you when you told them someone was trying to kill you and they couldn't find any evidence to back up your story," he pointed out.

"So?"

"So do you think they'll believe you when you tell them you shot a man in your house five times and he still chased you?" he asked.

Lauren couldn't reply.

"Oh, they might," he answered for her. "At least until they check out your house and find no trace of a gun or a body or bullet holes in the walls. Then they'll laugh with you all the way to the hospital, no matter how many times you tell them you don't want to go there. That's what they'll do. They'll stick you in some psychiatric ward for evaluation, and you'll be nothing more than a sitting duck for that guy who wants you dead. Or, at the very least, they may start taking their time getting to your house when you call them."

She looked away finally, sick to her stomach, sick at heart, knowing there was no one she could trust to believe her. Colt was right. The killer had probably not left any evidence. Even the knife he'd used on Mav was her own. The police would probably think she'd stabbed her own dog.

He went back to bandaging her hand. "I've seen it happen before," he muttered. "The cops don't believe everything. It's easier that way. Especially when it comes to these small-town cops. The most some of them ever have to deal with are drunk drivers and stolen bicycles and rowdy tourists. You can figure that the excitement of that bank robbery where you were shot will probably last them the whole year."

The thought made Lauren shiver. "Do you do much work with the police?"

He paused a moment, throwing her an unreadable glance. "I used to be the police."

Lauren's brows raised in surprise. "When?"

Her question brought about a memory—she could see it in his expression. He finished with her hand, tearing the gauze so that he could tie it in place. When he looked at her again, his eyes held the haunted look she'd seen in his office. "About a hundred years ago," he muttered sardonically. He released her suddenly, as though her touch burned him. And he left her thinking she'd done something or said something terrible to him.

He moved to the door and looked out, his body tense, ready, on guard still.

She watched him, noting the way his muscles moved and flexed, pressing against the cotton of his clothes. He really did remind her of some sort of knight who'd ridden in to save the day. No, she told herself. Not a knight. A brave. An Indian warrior. All he needed was a horse, and the feathered headdress of a chief and war paint on his face. His chest should be bare, too. She glanced down at his chest, imagining it without his shirt.

She couldn't keep staring at him, she had to get her priorities straight. Her dog was probably dead, her home had been vandalized and her hand was still throbbing. Not to mention the fact that a crazed killer wanted her for his next victim.

Colt moved away from the door, grabbed the telephone and quickly dialed the police. Lauren listened to the sound of his voice as he reported that her dog was injured and probably on the loose. His voice echoed within her, its rich sound embedded in her soul.

Looking down, he seemed to just now notice the blood from Lauren's hand staining the front of his shirt. He absently pulled the garment away from his stomach as he talked on the phone, examining the bottom where he'd torn away the cloth to bandage her hand.

"Thank you," she heard him mutter, before he hung up the phone. He pulled the shirt over his head and, opening the cabinet under the sink, he threw it in the trash can that was kept there.

Lauren's vision of an Indian chief suddenly came to life as she stared at his bare chest. His skin was smooth, taut, and his muscles were defined.

She sucked in a breath, and her pulse quickened. He was everything she'd imagined, and more. She bit her lip and fought the urge to reach out and feel the smoothness of his tanned skin.

The sound of thunder rolled in, louder, closer. The storm that had threatened earlier now seemed upon them. Lauren started slightly at the noise.

"What do I do if the police won't believe me?" she asked, feeling slightly out of breath and wishing she could sound stronger.

For a long moment, he said nothing. He moved to the dresser near the bed and retrieved a clean shirt. He turned to face her after he buttoned it up, offering her a small shrug. "I don't know," he replied honestly. "I have to think about what our next move should be."

"*Our* next move?" she questioned.

"We're in this together," he said without hesitation, moving back to the door.

The room was quiet for a long moment. Then Lauren shook her head. "No. I hired you to check this man out, nothing more. And you've done your job. It's me he wants. I don't want you involved any more."

"I'm already involved. I'm staying with you," he said.

Something flickered in his eyes when he said that, and Lauren wondered just what he was thinking. "No. He might—" She couldn't finish the sentence.

"Kill me?" he filled in for her.

"Yes!" A touch of frustrated anger whistled through her, mixing in with all the other emotions churning inside her. He was gracious to help her, but she wasn't about to let him die for her.

"As I see it," Colt said, "this guy probably already wants to kill me for riding in and saving you. And you saw the way he hit me."

Lauren might have laughed at his choice of words about riding in and saving her—under different circumstances. But not now. Too much was at stake. "How can you be so calm about this?" She stood up, her anger filling her with new strength. "You talk about his wanting to kill you like he wants to take you to lunch or something.''

The look he gave her was hot enough to start a fire in her blood. "I'm staying calm because if I let myself grow hysterical like you're becoming, then I'm apt to do something stupid that might get us both killed. If we want to do the right thing here, Lauren, we've got to keep our heads. We've got to behave rationally. And if you don't think you can do that, Red, then I might as well take you back to your inn right now and let that guy finish you off.''

His words stunned her, erasing her anger in an instant. Her knees grew weak, and she was forced to sit down again. For a long moment, she didn't quite know how to respond. Absently she pushed her hair over her shoulder to her back, as though the action might get rid of it or change its color. "Don't call me Red," she said, her anger still evident, but not nearly as strong. "That maniac was going to cut my throat, for God's sake. And he probably killed Mav. I have every right to get hysterical.''

"Maybe you do," he muttered, turning back to the window.

"He knew you. He said you and he went back a long way.''

"Yes," was all Colt said in reply.

Her frustration grew. "And you knew him, too, didn't you? From the moment I showed you his picture in the newspaper clippings?''

He took a deep breath and let it out in a sigh, sounding tired. "I wasn't sure it was the same guy I thought it was.''

"And is it?" she questioned.

"I don't know. He looks like it and sounds like it, but I still find it hard to believe."

"But you're certain that he really wants to kill you, too, aren't you?" she asked.

It was a long quiet moment before he replied. "Yes, I am."

"You don't sound like you're afraid to die," she pointed out, thinking she just might be hitting on why his eyes looked so haunted most of the time.

He sighed heavily, not looking at her. "I just think dying's easier than living sometimes."

She chuckled, and his head snapped around, his eyes meeting hers at the sound.

"That's the stupidest thing I've ever heard," she said.

"Why?" he demanded. His voice was touched with his own anger, but his face remained devoid of emotion. He crossed his muscled arms over his chest in a defensive way, reminding her even more of his Native American blood.

"Because unless you've died, you'll never know if the two can even be compared. And I know that life can be really hard to take sometimes. We all get dealt cards that we don't want to play."

His eyes narrowed. "So you think this is some sort of a game, do you?"

"No, I don't," she replied. "But I do know that the whole time I was fighting with that killer, I never once thought of giving up, no matter how much easier it might have been."

He was quiet for a long moment, and seemed to be contemplating her words. He looked out the window once again. "It's nearly dark," he said finally. "And there's a storm rolling in. It looks like it could be a big one."

"Do you think he'll come here?" she asked.

"I don't know," he said, without looking at her. "But I think we should expect the worst. He'll have the advantage of darkness. We won't be able to see him coming."

"What do you think we should do?" she asked, her fear sneaking out in her voice.

"Even the odds." He pulled out his gun for the first time, opened the chamber and reloaded it.

"Do you think that will do any good?" she asked, looking at the gun. "It didn't seem to stop him before."

He finished reloading and flipped the chamber into place again. "It stopped him for a moment. And it gave us the time to get out of there," he told her.

"Maybe he was wearing a bulletproof vest," she said.

"Maybe," he replied softly, his voice telling her he didn't believe it. He reholstered his gun.

Shadows were filling the room with the approaching darkness. And those shadows brought about a chill that sent a shiver up Lauren's back. The wind was picking up, and Lauren could hear it whistling in the chimney. It was an eerie sound. She watched Colt, his form stable and strong in a room of moving, unpredictable shadows. He was gazing out the window, on guard, alert. She found herself wanting to stand close to him, to lean against him. "Why would he want to kill you?" he asked again, his words breaking through her desire.

She shook her head slightly. "I told you I don't know."

"Well, did he tell you anything at all as to why?" he asked.

"Nothing he said made any sense," she replied, her voice hardly louder than a whisper in the quiet room.

She went on to tell him how the man had said he would explain it later. "But I knew later I'd be dead and I wouldn't care about any explanations."

He turned to her for a brief moment. "You're right," he agreed. "That doesn't make any sense."

"You said you had information on him. What did you come to tell me?" she asked. She'd forgotten Colt's reason for visiting her until just now. She wanted to keep talking. She wanted to keep hearing Colt's voice. It gave her something to concentrate on so that she wasn't shivering. It gave her something to think about so that she wasn't wanting his arms around her, so that she wasn't remembering the way he smelled and the strong comfort of his back when she'd held on to him on his motorcycle. And it gave her something to hold on to that was more than just the cold terror that refused to leave her.

"I still have friends in the department."

"Here in Rock Hill?" Lauren interrupted.

His eyes met hers through the darkness, and Lauren could still see that dark fire burning. "No. In Los Angeles."

Questions flew through her mind. Los Angeles? He'd been a cop in Los Angeles? How did he ever end up in a little tourist town like Rock Hill, Illinois?

But before she even had the chance to open her mouth and ask those questions, he continued. "Anyway, I was able to access their computer and find out for certain who the guy in the pictures is."

Lauren's heart raced through her chest with his words. She was finally going to be able to put a name with the face that haunted her dreams. "Who is he?" she whispered.

"His name is Dillon Waters." Colt was still watching her closely, his eyes seeming to hold her, to pull her even closer to him.

"The name doesn't ring any bells," Lauren said after a long moment.

"And you don't have any idea why he'd want to kill you?" he asked.

Lauren shivered again. "I've already told you, no."

"Waters originally came from this area. Are you sure you've never seen him before?"

"I'm sure!"

"You don't remember him at all?"

She paused, remembering the familiar feeling that had swept through her when he first pressed his face against her kitchen window.

"You do remember him from somewhere, don't you?" Colt questioned when she didn't reply.

"I don't know!" Lauren snapped. Absently she rubbed her temple, trying to calm her nerves. "He seemed vaguely familiar when I first looked at him square in the face, but I just can't remember where I've seen him before. And maybe he just seemed familiar after seeing him when he robbed the bank."

He turned away for a moment and asked, "He's not an old boyfriend with a grudge?"

For a moment, Lauren thought Colt sounded just a little jealous, and she wished he was looking at her.

"No," she said again. "I'd have remembered him."

"What about when you were a kid?" he persisted. "In grade school?"

She shook her head again. "I grew up outside of Chicago. I didn't move to Rock Hill until six years ago," she explained.

The strong wind of the coming storm blew through the trees outside the cabin, casting moving shadows across Colt's handsome features.

"Did you really come all the way out to my house just to tell me his name?" Lauren asked. "You could have called. But, I must admit, I'm glad you did make the trip. Thank you for saving my life," she added softly.

He faced her squarely. "I came to your house because I wanted to see your face when I told you his name. I wanted to see if there was any sign that you recognized his name."

"Why?" She couldn't keep from asking.

"Because Dillon Waters, the Dillon Waters who looks just like the man in the pictures and just like the man who tried to kill you today, was killed six months ago in a shoot-out with police after a bank robbery. He's dead."

reading and interpret. At the same time she wanted to delay his leave by adding to the terror she already felt.

"After all, they wanted me out of the picture, and now—"

"Could you possibly hold yourself together for a little longer than two minutes, Colt? You're still talking riddles. Start over. Start from the beginning, and don't leave anything out."

"Oh, he asked were—"

CHAPTER THREE

"**D**ead?" Lauren's voice was hardly more than a whisper.

"Yes," Colt said, moving from his position by the window and drawing closer to her.

Was he finally seeing how desperately she needed the closeness of another human being, Lauren thought. No, she realized. It wasn't just any other human being that she needed. It was Colt. Only Colt. She trembled at her sudden understanding. She remembered the feel of his hands, and she wanted, needed, to feel the comfort of his touch on her again.

She had to clear her throat before she could speak. "Maybe the man who tried to kill me just looks a lot like this man Dillon Waters." The hope in her voice sounded lame even to her own ears.

There was no reassurance in Colt's hesitant reply. "Maybe," he said finally, the single word coming out slowly. "Except that he still knew who *I* was."

The terror and the darkness were closing in on Lauren, making it hard for her to breathe. Making it hard for her to think. She nearly laughed, remembering the way she'd told Colt she had every right to be hysterical. Now she recognized the feeling. She wanted to laugh and cry at the same time. She wanted more than just the touch of his hands. She wanted to fall into Colt's arms, to feel the comfort of the warmth of his entire body pressing against hers. At the same time, she wanted to slap his face for adding to the terror she already felt.

Most of all, she wanted out of this endless darkness.

"Could you turn on a light?" she asked. She was still fighting just to keep her voice from shaking, and she wondered if he could tell.

"No," he replied evenly.

"Why not?" She didn't fight to control those two words. They came out just as offensive as she'd meant them to be.

"It's all part of evening the odds," he explained, his voice calm. "If we can't see him, we're not going to make it easy for him to see us."

"Good God, does that mean we're going to sit here all night in the dark?"

"Yes, it does," he replied. His voice was still calm, but it had dropped an octave and sounded oddly seductive.

Lauren concentrated on her anger, the feeling so much easier to manage than the terror or the warmth tingling through her at the sound of his voice. "I don't like the dark," she said through clenched teeth.

"And I suppose you'd like to have Dillon Waters find you, instead?"

"Of course not," she snapped, and jumped to her feet. They stood face-to-face. She advanced on him, taking a step forward. And, to her amazement, he took a step back.

"Why don't you make us a pot of coffee," he said. "It's going to be a long night."

"And how am I supposed to see what I'm doing?" she asked in a sweetly sarcastic voice.

He let out a sigh and seemed to ignore her for a long moment. "I suppose you're just going to have to feel your way around. You'll find the can of coffee in that cabinet next to the sink. The coffeemaker is on the counter.''

Lauren glared at him with hostility. ''This is easy for you, isn't it? This waiting in the darkness?''

''No,'' he said, turning back to the window. ''It isn't.''

''Well, you sure could have fooled me,'' she said, her voice still laced with sarcasm. ''But then, I guess you have every right to be calm about this. It's not you he tried to kill today.''

''I wouldn't be so sure about that,'' Colt replied evenly, rubbing his jaw where Dillon Waters had hit him. The certainty in his voice sent a another wave of coldness up Lauren's spine and brought a halt to her next sarcastic remark.

''Why don't you just explain how you knew him, and he knew you, and why he hit you?''

''No,'' he replied. ''His attack on me was because of an old grudge. Right now I'm more interested in why he would want to kill you.'' The determined way he spoke was enough to tell her that she wasn't going to get any further explanation. ''If you don't want to fix the coffee, I will,'' he said after a moment of silence. ''And you can stand here at the door and watch.''

She moved closer to him, to his position by the door. She had to fight the urge to reach out and touch him. ''Watch for what?'' she asked, looking through the glass in the door. Her anger, along with her desire, had given her strength, and her legs no longer felt weak.

The darkness outside somehow wasn't quite as terrible as the darkness inside. She could see the rippling of the lake and the depth of the trees around. Moonlight sifted between the gathering clouds and reflected off the grass and the water and the boards of the deck just outside the back door. The sky lit up slightly with a crack of lightning in the distance. Thunder sounded again.

"Look for anything," he replied, moving away from her, putting distance between them, just when his warmth and manly scent had grown close enough for her to touch. "Movement. Anything out of the ordinary."

He walked to the counter, and Lauren heard him making the coffee. The sounds of the scoop dishing out coffee and the running of water touched her again with that sense of being normal, common. It was hard for her to believe that amid such everyday sounds, she and Colt were waiting for the arrival of a man who wanted to kill her. *Would you like a piece of cake with your coffee?* she thought sardonically. *Make sure you set an extra place for when the guest of honor arrives.* God, what was happening to her? She must be losing her mind from fear. On top of it all, she still wanted nothing more than to be in Colt's arms. She closed her eyes for a moment, trying to get ahold of her emotions.

"Tell me about the accidents," Colt said, his voice suddenly bringing her back to the present.

"Well," she said softly, "the first was six months ago. I was involved in a car accident while I was on my way to Oregon to visit friends. Some man crossed the median and hit me head-on. I nearly died." She corrected herself. "I did die."

"What do you mean?"

At his question, Lauren looked over her shoulder at him. The little red light on the coffeemaker glowed with great intensity in the darkness, but Colt's face was hidden in the shadows.

"They told me later that I had been clinically dead for almost four minutes. The paramedics didn't think they'd be able to revive me, but they never gave up. One of them actually came by my hospital room later to see me, because he was so surprised I was alive," she explained.

"How long did it take you to recover?" Colt asked. He was finally finished making the coffee. He stepped closer to her, his hesitation evident even in the darkness.

"Over two months, with all the broken bones. And while I was in the hospital, I was given the wrong medication and got even sicker."

Colt took another step forward, his face lit by the small amount of moonlight that filtered in through the back door's window. Lauren's gaze met his. So many things became clearer when she looked into his eyes. In their depths, she could feel her own heart beating, she could hear her breathing and feel her lungs filling with air. Looking into his eyes filled her with such exhilaration.

"That's why you hate hospitals." It was a statement, not a question. And the gentleness in Colt's voice melted into her, pulling her to him, attracting her in a way she'd never felt before.

She could only nod, remembering.

"That was the first incident?" he questioned, his voice still tender.

"Yes," she whispered after a long moment. Her throat was tight again, only this time it wasn't due to her recent brush with death. It was from the fear she had of Colt—and, worse, of herself, and the way her body was responding to him.

She fought to keep her hands at her sides and not reach out to touch him. She couldn't believe how much she wanted to touch him. But even more, she wanted to be touched *by* him. She remembered the gentle way he'd cleaned her cut and covered it with a bandage. Looking down at her injured hand, she realized that the bandage hadn't just been slapped on to stop the bleeding. No. Colt had taken his time, and done the job with a great deal of care. She had the feeling he'd touch the rest of her body with just as much tenderness.

"And what about the school-bus incident? How were you involved?" he asked. His voice was soft, and Lauren wondered just how tight *his* throat was feeling.

"The bus crossed over the highway right in front of me," explained Lauren, trying to think of the accident and not Colt. "Then it went off the road to avoid hitting me."

He shrugged lightly, and Lauren noticed the way his muscled shoulders seemed to ripple with the movement. Again—only this time in her mind—she saw him without his shirt. She could see his muscled arms and hard chest.

"What happened? Did it go out of control?"

His question brought her back to reality but didn't wash away her desire to feel his touch. "I don't know. The driver was killed, so no one ever knew what really happened with him. Two of the kids were killed, too," she said softly, tears filling her eyes at the memory. "Some of the children said the driver was fighting over the wheel with another man."

In the dim light, Lauren could see Colt's eyes narrow. "But there wasn't another man on the bus?" he asked.

"No. No other adult was discovered after the accident. And no one ever came forward," she replied, still unable to look away from his eyes. Somewhere inside her she heard a voice that kept telling her she should turn back to the window. But she couldn't seem to break the hypnotic spell of Colt's gaze. A few steps closer and she'd be able to fall into his arms.

"You weren't hurt?"

Was that true concern in his voice or just simple curiosity? Lauren couldn't tell, but that gentleness, that unmistakable tenderness, was still there, pulling at her.

She shook her head. "The bus missed me entirely."

Colt's gaze shifted to the coffeemaker, and the spell was broken. "I think the coffee's ready. Care for a cup?" he asked.

Lauren was able to breathe on her own again, and she looked outside. "Yes, thank you," she muttered, her words sounding slightly out of breath. "Just sugar," she added.

"What about the hotel fire?" he asked. His back was turned to her while he poured the coffee. His voice took on a husky tone.

He brought a cup to her, and their fingers touched as he transferred the cup to her hands. His touch seemed as hot as the coffee itself, and for a moment Lauren thought the cup might slip from her grasp. She looked up at him again, searching for that hot black fire she'd fallen into before, but his gaze was now hidden in the shadows.

She had to clear her voice again before she could speak. "Sometimes during the year, mostly after the holidays, when I have a few days between guests at the inn, I visit other inns and hotels, just to compare their quality and hospitality to mine. And to see if there's anything I could add at my inn that would make my guests feel more welcome. Back right after the first of the year, after I'd finally healed from the car accident, I was staying at a place called the Hotel Williamstown, when it caught fire. I had to escape through a window and jump into a safety net."

"Do you know what caused the fire?" He asked as if he were a teacher posing a test question.

"No, but you do, don't you?"

He moved nearer—close enough that Lauren could sense his now-familiar masculine scent. Yet he didn't give her a second glance. He looked past her out the back window. "It started in the kitchen," he said. "And was deliberately set."

"How do you know that?" she asked. "I could never find anyone who would tell me about that investigation."

"I did a lot of checking during the last few days," he replied absently. He looked at her, and the expression in his eyes softened.

A woman could melt in a look like that, she thought. She forced her gaze away from his, wondering if he knew how well he could make her forget her problems. Yes, Colt Norbrook probably did know what a heartbreaker he could be.

"So it was arson," she said. "But there must have been hundreds of people staying in that hotel. Any one of them could have been the target. It didn't necessarily have to have anything to do with me."

"Maybe," he replied.

"You know more, don't you? You know a lot more than you're telling me."

He was quiet for a long moment, confirming her suspicions, and Lauren fought the urge to throw her coffee in his face. "If you don't tell me, I'll—"

"You'll what?" he questioned, his voice low, almost seductive, and laced with just a hint of amusement.

Good God, she thought, he was toying with her. "I'll kill you myself, that's what," she replied evenly. He wanted to test her limits? Fine, she'd show him just how close to the edge she was.

His brows rose quizzically at her statement.

"You don't think I will?" she asked, still working to keep her voice even. "I've already shot Dillon Waters. Shooting you probably wouldn't be too hard."

He stared at her for a long moment, and Lauren was certain he was going to laugh. He didn't. He turned away slightly, and she couldn't see his face, read his expression.

"I have copies of the hotel's security videotapes for the week of the fire," he finally said.

"Just how did you manage that?" she asked, her tone as determined as the look on her face.

"It pays to have friends in high places," he replied.

"Apparently."

"Most of the tapes from that day were burned up or melted because they were still loaded into the main recorders. But the others were stored in the basement and survived the fire," he explained, taking a casual sip of his coffee.

"So, are you going to tell me what was on them or are you just going to keep me in suspense?" she asked sarcastically.

"Dillon Waters checked into the hotel the day before the fire."

For a moment, Lauren thought her knees might give out beneath her. The anger disappeared in an instant, replaced by sharp, icy terror. Colt reached out and took her cup away from her. It was only then that Lauren saw that her hands were shaking.

"He even registered under the name Dillon Waters," Colt went on. "His name was in the computer records."

Lauren moaned. "If that's true, then you must be wrong about the bank robbery. There is no way he could have been in that hotel after he was shot by the police."

Colt was silent.

"*What is it?*" she asked through gritted teeth. "I know there's more you're not telling me. I can see it in your eyes. I can hear it in your voice. Why don't you just explain it to me? I'm riddled with questions, and I'd really appreciate it if you could answer a few right now."

"I can't," he said simply, finally turning his gaze to look at her. His words were soft, calm.

"You can't?" she shot back, her voice rising. "It's me he wants to kill and you stand there and tell me you can't tell me what else you know. Why not?"

"I just can't." He refused to meet her gaze. "All I can tell you is that I'm certain that a man who looks exactly like the man at your accident scenes, exactly like the man who tried to kill you today and who goes by the name of Dillon Waters, was shot by the police."

She wanted to cry. She wanted to scream in rage. "Well," she said, trying to control her voice, "just what more can you tell me?"

"Nothing. Yet."

She let out an angry sigh. "Well, *Mr.* Norbrook, you can go to hell." She moved past him, without any definite intentions. She just wanted away from him. Far enough away that his warmth didn't affect her. Far enough away that she didn't get lost in the darkness of his eyes and wish so much for the feel of his touch.

"I've already been there."

His words, and the quiet way he spoke them, stopped her. "What are you talking about now?"

He wasn't looking at her. He was looking out at the night, and Lauren got the distinct impression that he wasn't seeing the trees and the lake and the gathering storm out there. He was seeing something from his past. A memory of what he considered hell.

"Nothing." It was a long moment before he spoke that single word. And when he turned slowly to look at her, Lauren could see his eyes glistened with—what? Unshed tears? And that haunted look was back full force.

"Colt, why is it so hard to get answers out of you?" she asked softly. "It's what I hired you to do. It's your job."

"And I'd be able to do my job if I knew exactly what it is we're dealing with here," he snapped. "But all I know is that we were attacked by a man who is supposed to be dead, and I'm finding it hard to accept. And then there's the question of why."

"I already told you—"

"That you don't know," he finished for her. "I heard you. And, lady, if there's something you're not telling me, something you're keeping from me, then you're not doing your job, either. And it might just get us both killed."

The room was quiet for a long moment as the two of them stared at one another, each seeming to search the other for answers and finding none. Why? she asked herself. Why had she had to meet Colt like this, under these circumstances? Why couldn't he have stayed at her inn, where she could have gotten to know him, at a time when there wasn't a killer after her?

"Get some rest," he suggested, his voice gruff.

Lauren blinked at him in confusion, not understanding his sudden, angry distance, not understanding the loss of her own anger.

"It's going to be a long night. I'll take the first watch, and I'll wake you in a couple of hours." He turned away again, as though he'd decided he'd already allowed her to see too much of his feelings.

At first, she wondered just how he expected her to rest. Then, the more she thought about it, the more she found the idea of sleep absolutely wonderful. "All right," she agreed.

"Not in the bed." His voice stopped her, as she began to cross the room to the sleeping area. But it was not his words that stopped her, it was the gruff, husky tone to his voice. Did it bother him so much that she was planning to sleep in his bed?

She looked at him for a long moment before replying, searching, waiting. "Why not?" she asked lightly. He made no move toward her. Instead, he reached behind him to set his empty cup on the counter. And it took all her will to remain where she was and not move back toward him.

The battle of wills clashed with the silence of the room. Then the room brightened with another flash of lightning, and Lauren could see clearly the battle raging within him. He clenched his fists at his sides, then crossed his arms over his chest again. And yet the look in his eyes, the expression on his face, gave him away. In a split second, she saw what he was trying to hide.

He wanted her.

His desire was plain and simple. And it caused her heart to race faster than it had during any of today's close calls.

Then Colt turned away, shutting her out once more, leaving her cold. "I want you over by the fireplace," he said.

"Wh-what?" she stammered, still staring at his back.

"By the fireplace."

Dear God, she thought, she'd escaped one maniac only to spend the night in a dark cabin with another. "On the floor?"

"Yes."

He wouldn't even show her the courtesy of looking at her when he spoke.

"On the bed, you'll be cornered," he explained. His voice sounded softer, and Lauren wondered what expression his eyes now held. "Next to the fireplace, you'll have a door on either side of you. If he comes in the back, you can escape out the front and vice versa."

She stood where she was. "You really think he'll come here, don't you?"

"I just don't want to underestimate him again," he replied.

"Again?"

He ignored her question and went on. "Not knowing the reason he wants to kill you puts us at enough of a disadvantage."

When Lauren realized that he wasn't going to say any more, she slowly turned toward the fireplace. She sat down on the floor beside it, leaned against it, resting the side of her face against the cool stones and closed her eyes. She crossed her arms around herself and worked to ward off the shiver that moved through her.

A warm human touch caused her eyes to open abruptly. She gasped and turned, meeting Colt's heated gaze. He was standing over her. With a gentleness she would never have expected, he placed a quilt around her shoulders and drew it around her. She was unable to tear her gaze from his. The two of them remained fixed, eyes holding, souls touching. Then Colt bent down on one knee in front of her, bringing them face-to-face.

Tentatively, as though he were afraid that if he touched her she might shatter into a thousand pieces, he slowly curled a lock of her hair around his finger. She could feel his eyes on her as he studied her intently. He drew closer. Lauren couldn't move, couldn't even breathe. His lips touched hers with the warmth and softness of velvet. It was a simple touch, just a brush of his lips. But in that single moment, fire surged through her.

Then, suddenly, he tore himself away and stood up.

"Colt?" she whispered, feeling bare after the way his eyes had taken her in and the fire of his kiss had burned through her.

"Yes, Red?"

She bit her lip hesitantly, knowing that with her next words she was either going to cross a bridge or burn it. "Why did you stop?"

He was still watching her closely, his expression carefully masked. He swallowed hard. After a long moment, he slowly replied, "I don't deserve you."

Lauren stared up at him. His words made no sense. How could he know he didn't deserve her? "What?" she whispered.

"Get some rest," he ordered before turning away.

She stared at his back as he walked away. She briefly thought of telling him again to stop calling her Red, but the truth was, the nickname sounded nice coming from his lips.

Closing her eyes, she tried to do as he'd instructed and moved to pull the quilt tighter around her. She gasped as pain shot down her shoulder at her movement.

Colt turned back to her in an instant. "What is it?"

"My shoulder," she muttered, rubbing it.

He knelt down before her. "What's wrong with it?"

He was so close that for a moment Lauren couldn't remember just what had happened to cause her pain. "The door," she remembered, unable to look away from him. "Dillon Waters hit me with the door when I was trying to escape. I must have moved too quickly or something just now."

"Did your shoulder hurt before?" he asked quietly.

"No, only just now, when I twisted to get a better hold on the quilt."

"Let me take a look."

"I think it'll be all right," she told him. The last thing she needed was to have him looking at her any more intently than he already was. "Besides, you'd need to turn on a light to see it."

"Then I'll turn on the bathroom light. Come on." He reached down gently and pulled on her uninjured arm, hauling her to her feet. Lauren had no choice but to go with him. The quilt slid off her and fell to the floor.

They walked over to the bathroom door, where he switched on the light, its brightness causing her to squint.

"Where does it hurt?" he questioned.

Lauren rubbed the outside of her left shoulder. "Here."

"You're going to have to unbutton your blouse so I can see it," he said, his voice low, harsh and husky. When she hesitated, he went on. "Lauren, if you're hurt, we have to see how bad it is. We have to take care of it so that it doesn't put us at a further disadvantage later."

Lauren knew he was right, but unbuttoning her blouse for him wasn't easy, not with the way the cut on her hand throbbed. And not with the way she could feel his eyes, his heat.

Her hand went to the first button, and she tried to draw in a breath, tried to keep her body from responding. But it was impossible. Her breasts already pushed uncomfortably against the fabric of her bra.

"Lauren, I just want to look—" His words sounded breathy. "At your shoulder."

Yes, she thought, but opening her blouse would give him the chance to see so much more. The second button popped free, then the third. The air that touched her exposed, hot flesh felt cool. She released the fourth and final button, and held her breath. Slowly she moved her blouse away to reveal her shoulder.

Colt grasped the fabric, as well, to help her, sliding it away quickly, as though he could no longer stand the suspense. His knuckles swept across the smooth, flawless skin at her collarbone, and she shivered at the sudden heat that filled her at his touch.

In the light of the bathroom, he could see all of her. Standing at her side as he was, he'd be able to see the white lace of her bra, and the outline of everything underneath.

She forced herself to let out her breath, and then cursed herself for holding it in the first place. In the quiet room, it sounded almost as if she were panting, and her breasts rose and fell, pushing against her bra with each breath.

The hot touch of his fingers, as he moved her bra strap lower, out of the way, caused heat to race through her. His fingertips gently touched her shoulder gently as he examined her.

"You've got a hell of a bruise," he said finally, his voice sounding strained. "But I don't see anything else to indicate it's something worse."

When he finally took his hand off her shoulder, Lauren quickly slipped her blouse back up and worked the buttons. She still couldn't look at him. She knew that if she saw those dark fires burning in his eyes she'd never get the buttons of her blouse done up again. No, she'd be falling into his arms, begging to have his hands touching her everywhere.

"Try to get some rest now," he said, his voice even gruffer than before. He switched off the light, throwing them both into the darkness.

"Colt?" she said softly.

"What?" He hadn't moved a muscle since he let her go and switched off the light. He was still at her side, still so close she could feel his warmth. Or was that the warmth of her responding to him?

"Nothing," she said quickly. "Thanks for checking it out."

Working to get her breathing under control, she moved back to the fireplace. Sitting, she pulled the quilt around her, slowly and carefully this time. She tried to rest, but found she couldn't even relax. It was impossible to get the memory of Colt's touch out of her mind.

She opened her eyes after a moment to watch Colt. He was pacing the room slowly, silently, always watching, waiting, on guard. What an enigma the man was, she thought, wondering just what made him tick. What could have happened to him to make him so withdrawn? What a challenge it would be to find out. She knew there was tenderness in him, just waiting to get out. She smiled softly in the darkness, glad to be thinking about something other than the attempt on her life, glad to feel something other than fear, even if it was a longing she didn't think would ever be fulfilled. But even as withdrawn as he was, she knew she could depend on Colt to help her. He had to. She had no one else. And maybe after this was over, after they were both safe...

She stopped her train of thought, knowing she had no chance with Colt Norbrook. He didn't trust her, he hadn't believed her when she'd said she didn't know why Dillon Waters would want to kill her. And that wasn't the way to start off any kind of relationship.

But, trust or no trust, the fact was, she was still attracted to him. She still wanted him as she'd never before wanted a man.

She didn't know she'd drifted off to sleep until she awoke abruptly, thinking for a moment that someone had called her name. She felt an immediate sense of fear, a sudden awareness of danger that prickled up her spine.

The storm was blowing full force, thunder and lightning doing battle in the sky. Looking toward the back door, she saw Colt crouched low beside the hinges, his gun held up and ready. Her gaze shifted to the glass.

A sudden flash of brightness illuminated *him*—Dillon Waters. He stood outside the door, his face just on the other side of the window.

Eyes filled with strong, deadly confidence, he was looking right at Lauren.

CHAPTER FOUR

"Colt?" Lauren whispered. Her throat was tight, the single word coming out painfully. She wasn't able to draw in a breath, and a wave of terror washed through her.

"Don't make a sound," he whispered back, his voice harsh. He was tense, ready to spring. He never looked at her. He was staring at the door beside him. He pulled the hammer back on the gun he held ready, the sound of it echoing loudly in the room.

Lauren shifted her gaze to Dillon Waters. He stood just on the other side of the door. His gaze caught hers and held it. There was a small, easy smile on his lips that Lauren found confusing. He didn't look like a man who had any intention of killing. He looked like a man who might be stopping in for a few drinks and some enjoyable conversation.

And Lauren couldn't take her eyes off him.

Then a voice from somewhere close to her said *Relax, Lauren.*

To Lauren's amazement, she was able to relax. It wasn't nearly as hard to do as she'd thought it would be.

More words came to her. *I love you, Lauren.*

She found the idea of being loved reassuring, warming. She was vaguely aware of the quilt sliding from her shoulders. She no longer needed it. She tried to turn her head, to see where the voice was coming from.

No, don't look away.

She didn't. It was so much easier to look at Dillon Waters, anyway.

Come closer, Lauren, the voice ordered gently. *Come to me. You are my love.*

She lifted herself from her stooped position, her body sliding slowly up the cool stones of the fireplace. She hesitated only a moment, to let the renewed circulation in her legs take away the shaking and weakness there.

Dillon's eyes bore into hers, pouring warmth into her, filling her with calm and contentment. *Come to me, love.*

She stepped closer. He was what she needed. She knew that now. She didn't know why she had ever trusted Colt Norbrook. Except for a few glimpses of gentleness here and there, he hadn't given her any warmth. He hadn't even let her get within three feet of him before he moved away, saying stupid things like he didn't deserve her.

That's right, Lauren. Dillon Waters's voice was coming to her again. *Norbrook doesn't deserve you. He doesn't love you. He isn't capable of loving anybody.*

Lauren smiled softly, and wondered just how he was able to talk to her so clearly when he never even moved his lips.

But I love you, Dillon continued. *You are my heart. You belong in my soul.*

How poetic, she thought. How romantic. Lauren stepped even closer, moving silently toward the door.

You have to let me in, said Dillon. *I can't get in unless you unlock the door, love. Then I can love you as I know you want me to.*

Lauren nodded. Yes, she did so much want him to love her. There was nothing so wonderful as being loved.

That's right, Dillon murmured. *But first you have to get past Norbrook. He'll stand between us. He'll try to stop me from loving you.*

Lauren glanced at Colt just in time to see him slide himself up the wall until he was standing, poised and ready, beside the door. He was still watching the door, and he didn't know she was coming toward him. Nor did he seem to hear Dillon's voice as Lauren did. Her eyes again met Dillon's through the glass.

That's right, love. Norbrook can't hear me. My voice is only for you, my words are only for you.

I don't want to hurt him, she thought. He helped me, I just can't quite remember how.

I know, said Dillon. *You don't have to hurt him. Just get to the door, just unlock it. And I'll make sure he doesn't stop me from loving you.*

She was almost there. Nearly to the door. Colt, and the door, were only a few feet from her. Two or three more steps and she'd be able to reach out and grasp the lock.

That's it, love, keep coming. You're almost there. Just keep thinking about how I'll be able to touch you. Come quietly. Now, before I have to leave. I'll distract Norbrook for you.

He brought his fingers up to the glass and tapped lightly, keeping Colt from noticing Lauren.

Lauren was close enough to reach the lock, and still Colt didn't know she was there. He was too caught up in watching the door, expecting Dillon Waters to come crashing through it.

Do it now, love! Do it quickly!

She reached out to unlock the door, and her hand came into Colt's line of vision.

"Lauren!"

She knew he'd shouted out her name, but he sounded so far away.

Dillon's voice was louder, so much louder, so loud it was giving her a headache. *Do it, Lauren! Don't let him stop you! Don't let him stop me from loving you!*

She got her hand to the doorknob, and then Colt's hand closed over hers. "Lauren, what the hell are you doing?"

"I have to let him in," she explained. "He can't get in unless I unlock the door."

Turn the lock, Lauren! Dillon was yelling at her, and the sound was hurting her ears.

"He needs me to unlock the door!" she screamed at Colt, yelling over Dillon's voice.

Colt was so much bigger than she, so much stronger. His hand refused to let her turn the lock. She looked into Dillon's eyes through the glass. So close. He was so close. His love, his warmth. It was all so close, and yet she couldn't touch it. "He loves me," she said softly. "I need him."

"No, Lauren. He wants to hurt you."

Colt's voice was so soft, so gentle, and it was still so far away. But Lauren knew he was lying to her. It was just as Dillon said. Colt was trying to keep them apart.

"No. He could never hurt me." She stared at Dillon, feeling his love. "He loves me."

"Lauren?" Colt was pulling her hand from the doorknob, his voice filled with confusion. "What's wrong with you?"

You have to let me in, Lauren. I can't go in to any dwelling unless the door is opened or I'm invited.

Like a vampire, she mentally questioned. She wasn't afraid and suddenly felt like laughing. Dillon's chuckle reached her.

Yes, love. Something like that. It's just that all my energies are focused on you. Smash the glass, came Dillon's voice, strong but gentle, filled with that loving warmth she needed so much. *If you break the glass, I can get in to you, my love.*

Lauren raised her other hand without thought. Dillon stepped out of the way.

In the same instant, Colt realized what was happening. "My God, he's got you hypnotized!" His gun still in his hand, he wrapped his arm around her waist and pulled her bodily to the floor before she could make contact with the glass.

She fought him, trying to bring her knee to a vulnerable place while attempting to slither out from under him. "No!" she cried out. "I have to let him in! He loves me!"

Somewhere behind all her screaming, she heard Dillon's voice, so loud and clear he might have been standing right over her. *Have no doubts, love. I'll be back for you.*

Lauren saw Colt set his gun down a short distance away so that he could hold her with both hands. She reached for the weapon, but he stopped her. Then, gripping both her wrists, he held them above her head as she writhed and twisted beneath him, trying to escape him.

Colt slapped her. His palm whizzed across her cheek, leaving a trail of instant heat. She felt a rush of blood come to her face, and her cheek burned.

And everything stopped. The voice, the feeling of love, the warmth. All of it disappeared in an instant, leaving nothing but an indescribable weakness, that hot pain in her face, and a coldness that washed through the rest of her.

She looked up at Colt, who was lying on top of her, still holding her hands above her head, his eyes meeting hers. Through the weakness, the cold terror and the lingering pain in her cheek, she shivered. The hand that had been cut before throbbed painfully, and her shoulder was hurting, as well.

She looked up at Colt. He grew blurry from the tears that filled her eyes. She drew in great gulps of air and panted, trying not to let go of the sobs she felt building inside her.

"What—what happened?" she gasped, finding it hard to speak.

"He hypnotized you," Colt replied shortly. Releasing her hands, he glanced away to take in the window at the back door.

Lauren followed his line of vision, a wave of nausea rising up in her, forcing her to take a deep breath and swallow it down.

Dillon Waters was gone.

Lauren didn't know if she liked the idea. True, if he was gone, she didn't have to look at him. At the same time, she didn't know where he was. He might be lurking right outside, waiting for the right time to try something else to get to her. Or was he miles away by now?

Colt remained perfectly still, watching her, testing her to see just what she would do next, now that Waters was gone. Good God, he'd never seen anything like that in all his years on the force. Lauren had been completely dazed, completely under Dillon Waters's control, and if he hadn't known better, he would have thought she'd been drugged.

He was still stretched out on top of her, and he could feel every curve of her body beneath him. The heat of her coursed through him, and he cursed his own response to her. He didn't want her like this, not when only minutes before she'd been completely under Waters's command. He looked down at her, grateful to see her eyes clear. She was drawing her breaths in quickly and harshly, and her breasts pushed up against his chest with each breath. His face was merely inches from hers. If he moved any lower, he could kiss her again. He almost shook his head to clear it, knowing that if he did kiss her, there would be no stopping after that. He had to get off her now.

Colt sat up suddenly, clearing his throat and working to control his own breathing. He retrieved his gun, pressing the safety catch before sliding it into his shoulder holster. His gaze moved back to her. "Lauren..."

Lauren looked up at him. She was still fighting tears, still fighting to calm her breathing. "I was going to let him in, wasn't I." But it was a statement, not a question.

"Yes."

Lauren didn't fight the sobs any longer. Tears slid down her cheeks. "Why is he doing this to me? Why?" she moaned. "Why me?"

Colt had no more answers than Lauren, and he said nothing.

She looked up at him with tear-filled eyes. "Will you hold me? Will you just hold me?"

How could he refuse her? And yet he knew that if he took her in his arms, he might never be able to let go. "Come here," he said softly, pulling her into his arms.

Lauren fell against him without hesitation, and she pressed her face into his shoulder, relishing the feel of him, the closeness of him.

Strange memories came to her, causing her to question the feel of his arms around her. For just a moment, she thought it was Dillon Waters holding her. Then her vision cleared, and it was Colt's arms that held her. All this time, she'd thought Colt was pushing her away from him. Well, he wasn't now. He was holding her, comforting her.

But he can't love you.

The thought confused her, and she didn't understand why such a thing enter her mind. Love was not a concern right now. She just needed the touch of another human being. Colt's touch. Only Colt's touch. And he was here, touching her, holding her. In his arms, she found everything she'd imagined—his warmth, his tenderness, his gentleness.

Colt held her close, her palms pressed against the muscled hardness of his chest. Everything about her touched his senses. His fingers brushed the softness of her hair, and he could feel the warmth of her skin beneath her blouse. He thought he could almost hear her heart beating—or was it his own heart? He couldn't be certain. He was sure of only one thing—the feel of the woman in his arms. And Dillon Waters or no Dillon Waters, control or no control, he had never felt anything so right in his life. He held Lauren even closer, knowing he had been right before. He didn't want to let her go. Not now. Not ever.

Lauren was finally able to bring her tears under control, but she didn't move away from Colt. And he didn't release her, just leaned away slightly, and Lauren had to fight the urge to cling to him.

"At least we know we're safe as long as the doors are locked," Colt said.

"We do?" That immense confusion washed over her again.

"Yes. He couldn't get in unless you unlocked the door for him."

"Oh," was all she could think to say in reply. Nausea washed over her at the thought of how close she'd come to letting him in. "He couldn't break the glass, either."

"How do you know?" Colt asked.

She tried to remember but thoughts only seemed to swirl in her mind. Thoughts that made no sense. Thoughts of vampires and energies and things that would give Colt reason to think she'd totally lost her wits if she revealed them. "I don't know," she answered finally. "But I was going to break the glass for him, wasn't I?"

He nodded before pulling her close again.

The room was quiet. For a long moment, there was only the sound of their breathing, the fall of rain and the rippling of the wind blowing the lake and trees outside.

"So he's not a man, is he?" she asked. "He really is dead, and he's some sort of a ghost that isn't able to go through walls or doors."

"I don't know, Lauren," Colt said, his voice rough. "It's all pretty hard to phantom."

She forced a chuckle at his choice of words. "What are we going to do? I mean, if he really is some sort of a ghost, how do we get rid of him?"

"I don't know yet. But I think we could both use some rest right now."

Lauren shifted in his arms to look back at the fireplace, where she'd slept before.

"No," he said, answering her unspoken question. "In the bed this time." He pulled her slowly to her feet, never letting go of her hand.

"Together?" She shivered. The thought of being with him in the bed was almost too much to handle on top of everything else she'd experienced. She knew that if she was that close to him, she'd never get any rest, no matter how exhausted she was.

"Yes." He was leading her to the bed.

"But what if he comes back and hypnotizes me again. I might...do something." What if she hurt Colt? What if she managed to put her hand through one of the windows? Just thinking about it made her dizzy with fear. And knowing Colt was going to be in the bed with her didn't help. His hard body was going to be close. The inviting masculine scent of him would be all around her. On the sheets. On the pillow. On him. And what would happen if, no—when she reached out to touch him? Because now that she'd been in his arms, she found she didn't want to leave them. She wanted to find out where his holding her and touching her might lead.

"Sit down, Lauren," he ordered gently when they had reached the bed. He turned down the comforter and gave her a slight push, to set her on the sheets.

Lauren sat quietly, feeling as though she were somehow invading his private domain. The mattress sank beneath her and the sheets felt so cool, so smooth and inviting against her hands.

"Now lie down," he directed.

She started to protest. "I—"

Lightning struck, and the sudden brightness of it briefly illuminated the room through the window. Lauren started at the closeness of the sound of thunder that followed.

"It's all right." He calmed her with his voice, his hand tenderly touching her shoulder. "Don't be afraid of the storm. I'll light a candle for you, okay? It should be all right. Lie down and face the wall."

Lauren heard him strike a match, and then the room was lit with a faint light. He put the candle back on the nightstand where he'd found it and the matches, and his eyes moved to Lauren's. There was a tenderness such as she'd never seen before in those dark, endless depths.

She couldn't believe the intensity with which she wanted the man before her. It built up in her like a growing fire that had started in the pit of her stomach and was now spreading like molten lava through the rest of her. She didn't know him, and yet, looking in his eyes, she saw eternity. She saw everything she ever needed to know.

And she saw his desire for her. It was enough to cause her heart to quicken, sending blood and heat pulsing through her body, more quickly than ever before.

Colt could feel the heat of her gaze. Her hair cascaded down over her shoulders like a dark fire fall, and he longed to bury his hands in it. His fingers still tingled with sparks from touching the smoothness of her flesh, and he wanted more than anything to touch her again.

He reached up slowly to cup her cheek with his palm. His thumb brushed against her lower lip, the light caress reaching all the way to her heart. The strength in his hand was unmistakable. She was drawn to it, and she turned her head slightly toward it. Yet it was the tenderness, the quiet compassion that radiated from him, that struck with nearly the intensity of the lightning that had flashed moments before.

But he can't love you. He can't love anybody.

The voice seemed to be coming from inside her own mind. And just hearing it brought back the fear. Yes, he can, she thought, her conscious mind arguing with the unknown voice. She had felt too much in the kiss they'd shared. She had felt caring in his hands when he bandaged her cut and examined her bruise.

But that's not love. You'll see.

She had no time to argue again, for Colt was leaning down toward her now. "Destiny be damned," he muttered. His breath on her face was warm, inviting, promising.

Lauren was given no chance to comprehend the meaning behind his words. For, at that moment, his lips touched hers. The contact was warm and utterly delicious and perfect, harder than that brush of a kiss before. And it shook her very being. His mouth moved over hers expertly. Wanting, needing, giving all at once.

It was more than just a kiss. So much more. It was a claim, a brand, a seal. It made her his. If only for this single moment in time, she was his, and only his.

She took what he offered and returned what she had, responding, moving with him, following his lead. At his command, her lips parted even more to allow his tongue inside.

He touched her with the promise of how much more there could be.

She let that promise hold her. She let it take her. She used it to push away the shadow of doubt, to push away that inner voice.

His palms moved to just below her jaw, his fingers spanning the soft flesh of her throat. He held her tightly to him, as though he was afraid she would slip away.

She wanted to tell him that he didn't have to worry about her slipping away from him. She wasn't going anywhere.

Still that little voice nagged at her, sounding angry now. And, as if in reply, the room was brightened again by a crack of lightning that was followed by the roar of thunder.

Don't do this, Lauren. I'll be very angry.

Lauren almost pulled away at that threat, and for a moment she thought someone behind her had actually spoken the words.

Then Colt's tongue probed still further, the sensation of it pushing the voice aside, taking her away to some warm, safe place where there was room only for the two of them.

His kiss left her lips, moving slowly over her face to her jaw and the softness of her neck. "Oh, Lauren," he whispered, his voice harsh and ragged. "I need you. I need you so much...." He quickly took off his shoulder holster and gun and set them on the small table beside the bed.

She understood his need. He'd awakened the same feeling in her. Her hands moved around him, clutching his shirt.

He grasped her shoulders and gently, ever so gently, eased her back onto the bed. Slowly he reached for the buttons of her blouse. He opened each one gently, giving his fingers time to brush against the soft flesh underneath. Giving her time to acknowledge every touch, every caress. His mouth moved to just below her ear, tickling her softly, and a shiver passed through her.

She moved her hands to the front of his shirt and pulled as hard as she could. She didn't think her hand was up to twisting each button, and she didn't want to take the time to open each one, as he was hers. She needed to feel the warmth of his chest. She needed to see him as she had before, when he changed his shirt, as she had in her mind. She needed skin touching skin, living flesh, touching living flesh right now.

No, Lauren!

"Yes!" she screamed at the voice.

Colt raised up slightly, meeting her eyes. "Yes?" he questioned softly, thinking she was merely confirming her need for him.

"Yes," she repeated, holding his gaze.

His shirt pulled free, and she put her hands on his warm, solid flesh. He had her shirt open in the same instant, and his hands touched her with all the intensity of hot coals. She gasped and arched against him, and the angry voice she had heard faded away to nothing.

His mouth returned to hers for a moment, tasting her, taking her, possessing her. At the same time, as if by some quick magician's trick, he removed her bra. His hands then had access to the softness of her breasts. She groaned at the spark his touch set off inside her.

Slowly, tantalizingly, he undid the rest of her clothing, kissing every place he exposed.

Lauren tried to do the same to him, but the cut on her hand made it impossible for her to unbutton his jeans. But that didn't slow them down. He helped her. And when there were no more clothes between them, he moved over her, between her thighs.

She wanted him. She needed him. She was moving against him.

Then something stopped her.

He must have felt her tense, for he suddenly stopped his seduction. "What is it? Don't tell me you're having second thoughts," he murmured teasingly.

"Someone's in here. I can feel them watching," she whispered.

He glanced around. "There's no one here," he replied softly. "It's just you and me, Red. And, oh, are you beautiful...." His last words came out breathy. In the same instant, he slipped into her warmth.

From there on, he showed her that he *could* love her. He drove her to the edge of the sane world as she knew it. He loved her with every caress, every kiss, every movement. He filled her with himself, showing her more love than she had ever thought she could possess.

His movements grew forceful, hungry, filling her with fire. She held on to him, matching his rhythm, clinging to him as though she were riding the edge of the thunderstorm unleashing its fury outside the cabin. She let go. Let go and allowed the passion to take her away like the wind, to a place where the heat exploded within her. She cried out his name. "Colt!"

"Yes, Lauren. I'm right here, right here with you, all the way." His voice was so close to her. It took the place of that other voice, and she welcomed it.

He brought his lips to hers again, brought himself into her again and again. Making her his. A moan escaped him as he shuddered against her. "Why did I ever fight this?" he muttered.

"You fought this?" she asked, out of breath.

"Yes," he said. "Ever since that first time I saw you. When I crashed into you in the grocery store. I've been fighting wanting you like this." He could see now, feel now, that she was what he'd needed all along. She was the second chance that he'd thought he'd never get. She was what he'd needed to make him whole. To give him life....

For the first time in a very long time, he felt totally, utterly complete.

"Why did I ever think I had to push you away?" he muttered.

She smiled up at him. "Stupid thinking on your part," she replied, before pulling him toward her to touch her lips to his.

"Well, I'm glad you cured me of that problem."

"My pleasure." She paused. "You ran into me in the grocery store?" She couldn't help but ask. "When?"

He rolled over beside her, breathing heavily. Yet he still held her, as though he were afraid to allow any space between them. "It was weeks ago," he muttered. "I accidentally bumped my cart into yours."

She was quiet for a long moment, dragging her memory. Then she chuckled softly. "I remember now. You were buying two half gallons of ice cream," she said, remembering.

"I can't help it. I have very little willpower when it comes to things that taste good." And, as though to prove his point, he leaned down and leisurely kissed her.

"So why did you fight your attraction to me?" she asked, when his lips finally left hers.

"I didn't know anything about you, not even your name. I didn't know if you had a husband and a couple of kids waiting for you. God knows you were buying enough food."

She laughed. "It was for the inn."

"I didn't know that then. I had planned to find out all about you as soon as I got my office set up and running. Then in you walked, wanting to hire me before I could check *you* out."

They were both quiet for a long moment.

"What about now?" she asked. "Tonight? You said you didn't deserve me. Why?"

He leaned up, and in the soft candlelight, looked into her eyes, into her very soul. "Because you really don't deserve any of this. What happened between Waters and me happened a long time ago. Why he wants to kill you now, I have no idea. Nor do I know if his reason for wanting you is somehow connected with me." He paused, and a slow grin came to his lips. "But I do know about you and me—and this." He ran a caressing palm down the length of her stomach, down till he reached her most sensitive spot.

"I've never felt anything so wonderful," she confessed.

"Never?"

"Never."

He smiled down at her. "Well, hold on to me, honey, because it's not nearly over."

And, to her amazement, it wasn't over for a long time.

Afterward, he held her for a long time, listening to their breathing as it returned to normal, listening to the storm that raged outside and the rain that beat against the roof. He simply couldn't let her go. He'd been cold for a very long time. After experiencing her warmth, it seemed as if he'd been cold all his life, and he never wanted to let go of her again.

He casually wrapped his fingers in the fiery waves of her hair.

"What if he comes back?" she asked, her question invading his world of peace.

"He can't get in," Colt replied softly, placing a kiss to her temple. He hoped he was right. He had no desire to die, but he now felt that if it *was* his time to go, he could leave this life knowing Lauren had at least given him his sense of feeling back.

Shifting her in his arms, he moved to leave the bed. Instinctively she turned and grabbed his hand. "Where are you going?" she whispered, her voice harsh, her sudden fear evident.

"Just to check the windows and doors. Stay here and face the wall. Don't look out the windows." He gave her hand a squeeze before letting her go.

Lauren fought the urge to watch him. She turned on her side, studying the roughness of the logs that made up the wall of the cabin. Right in front of her, she could see the dark outline of a large knot in the log. Behind her, she could hear Colt moving around, touching things, jiggling a door here, a window there, testing everything to make sure the locks were secure.

She was cold without him, and she shivered beneath the blankets. She tried to ignore the throbbing that had returned to her hand. Then he returned, and he slipped into the bed behind her, and blew out the candle. Pulling her close, he wrapped his arms around her tightly.

"What if he tries to hypnotize me again?" she asked.

"I'm going to keep you facing this way, so that if he does look in, you can't see him. You won't be able to look into his eyes. And just in case something does happen, you have to crawl over me to get to the door." He paused. When he spoke again, his breath was warm on her cheek. "I don't plan on letting you get away that easily, Lauren Baker."

She smiled sadly in the darkness, wondering if he really had any choice in the matter. But she wanted to believe his words. She wanted the hope they brought her. He was right, wasn't he? Dillon Waters had no control over her unless she looked at him, right? Right. She convinced herself, and drifted off. Only to find just how wrong she really was.

CHAPTER FIVE

Lauren?

Lauren fought the whispered sound of his voice, wanting only to remain in the warm, safe state of sleep.

Lauren?

She let out a little sigh and snuggled closer to Colt. His hard, muscular thighs pressed against the softness of her buttocks. His arm was still around her waist, holding her up against him. His hand touched her stomach. She placed her hand on his and tried to drift away again.

Lauren? The whispered voice touched her again, sounding close to her ear.

"What is it, Colt?" she mumbled.

The only sound that came back to her was his deep, even breathing. The room was silent, the storm over.

Her stomach tightened, clenched in fear, and the thought of sleep left her in an instant. She opened her eyes quickly, and in the darkness was able to see the contours of the logs making up the wall in front of her. Terror filling her, she waited.

She didn't have to wait long. The voice came to her again, seeming to come from somewhere just over her shoulder. *Lauren?*

She recognized Dillon's voice, and she closed her eyes tightly against it, hoping she could will the voice to stop.

"Colt?" she whispered, her voice feeling raw. She needed his help. She had no idea how Dillon Waters had gotten in, but he was here, close. And she was so paralyzed with fear, she could do nothing more than whisper. She couldn't move. She was so numb with fear that she didn't even have the strength to turn her head.

Don't wake him, Lauren, Dillon warned her. *I'm already angry at you for letting him have you, and you'll have to make it up to me.* He paused. *Besides, he doesn't love. Not anyone. He simply can't. Thanks to me, he'll never love you.*

"But he—" Suddenly she wasn't so sure. Was what she'd shared with Colt nothing more than a good roll in the hay to him? Surely not. She thought he'd felt so much more. She wanted so much more. She wanted—

Her thoughts abruptly stopped as the face of Dillon Waters filled her mind. Behind her closed eyelids, she saw Dillon's face clearly. He was staring at her, reaching out to caress her cheek. She opened her eyes and saw nothing but the cabin's wall. A shiver washed through her when she felt the cool touch of something on her cheek. She jerked away, pressing her cheek into the mattress. Even that slight movement was in slow motion, and it took all her concentration to do it. Yet, to her horror, the cool feeling of his touch remained. "Leave me alone," she moaned, unsure whether she'd spoken out loud or merely thought the words.

I can't, replied Dillon. His voice was soft, seductive, and Lauren remembered the way he'd promised to kill her quickly and painlessly. *I love you. It's getting close to time for me to move on, and I don't want to go without you.*

"I don't love you," she told him. "Please leave me alone."

No.

"But I don't love you," she insisted.

You did. Once. Long ago. He paused. *I wish I could help you to remember.*

She closed her eyes tightly, wanting to shut him out, to eliminate the sound of his voice. She didn't want to hear any more.

But Dillon was there. When she closed her eyes, she could see him again. He was so close, his hand was still on her cheek. He was touching her in the same way, in the same place Colt had, just before he'd kissed her. Lauren tried to move away from his touch. She didn't want Dillon defiling her memory of Colt. But she couldn't get away from him. There was no place for her to go. His face was mere inches from hers. When he spoke, she could feel his breath. She could smell his breath, and the stench of it caused her stomach to lurch.

Her eyes snapped open and he was gone. The wall was before her again.

You can't escape me, said Dillon.

She could feel him caressing her cheek. She could feel the icy touch of his fingers. That feeling of near-paralysis never leaving her, she brought her hand up, trying to wipe away the feel of his touch. With her hand, she felt nothing on her face. And yet the coolness was still there....

Hot terror rose up in her, burning her throat, cutting off her breath. She choked, trying to breathe. Dear God, had his hand moved to her throat? Was he now choking the life out of her?

She couldn't tell.

Let me go, her mind cried out. She closed her eyes so that she could see him. He was strangling her, his fingers wrapped around her throat. She clawed at his arm, but her nails caught nothing but the sheets of the bed. She reached to scratch his face, and still grazed nothing.

She kicked out at him, but hit nothing but the sheets.

To add to her horror, she saw him smiling at her.

You see, my love? It happens in stages. Before I could not kill you outright. It had to be accidental. But then I moved to another stage, and I was able to touch you. Hold you. It would have been so easy to kill you with that knife. But I made a mistake in hesitating, wanting only to feel you in my arms. And now I have only to wait for you to cross into that place which is not yet sleep and not yet wakefulness, and you are here with me. You are mine.

No! Please! Why are you doing this to me? She wanted to cry out. Her mouth opened, but nothing could pass in or out of her throat. Her words were trapped. She was trapped.

Still, he answered her silent question. *I already told you. I love you. I want you with me.*

But you're dead.

Yes.

She shuddered at the confirmation. Already she could see spots before her eyes. Even though she knew it was doing no good to fight, she couldn't stop. She wouldn't let go so easily. She didn't want to die. Not when there was so much to live for. There was her inn, her horses. Colt.

She looked up at Dillon and saw his eyes darken. *Don't think of him. Not now. Think only of me. Look only at me. We will be together forever. Very soon.*

But Lauren was almost beyond thinking. The need for air was no longer so important.

Things were growing dark, even darker than the cabin....

She could, however, still see Dillon Waters smiling, filled with confidence. He'd won. He'd gotten to her, and she'd never had a chance.

But I don't love you, her mind cried out.

But you did. So long ago. I know it was only for a short time, but you will remember. I'll help you remember, he said, the smile never leaving his face. *You'll love me again. I promise.*

Another promise. The last thing she wanted from him was a promise. All she wanted was to breathe.

His grip on her throat tightened even more.

Then he leaned over her and touched his cold lips to hers. It was the kiss of death.

She fought with all the strength she had left. She tried to pull away, but her head was already pressed against something hard. Colt's chest?

Think of Colt, she said to herself.

No, said Dillon, his anger palpable.

Colt. Colt. She tried to call his name. She tried to picture his face in her mind. If she was truly going to die, then she wanted to die remembering him, remembering the way he'd made her feel when he made love to her.

Then suddenly something hard, something undefined, shook her. And from far away came another voice. "Lauren!" It was Colt's voice.

"Yes!" she tried to reply. "Help me!"

No! The single word came from Dillon, sounding like the growl of a wild animal. His grip tightened, and she was certain that any moment he was going to snap her windpipe in two.

Something shook her again. Hard. The force of it pulled her out of Dillon's grasp.

She gulped in a mouthful of air. That was all that mattered now. Breathing. Gulping in breath after breath, through a throat that was still tight, trying to make up for all that Dillon Waters had cut off.

She heard Colt's voice growing closer, calling her name, and knew that Dillon was moving away. Thank God, she thought. She clutched at her throat, where his fingers had just moments before threatened to end her life.

She watched Dillon, who was still moving away. The expression on his face was one she would never forget. It was an expression of pure, uncontrolled rage. His eyes bore into hers with such hostility that Lauren thought they might pop out of his head. Fury seemed to vibrate from him, touching her and sending chills throughout her body. She trembled uncontrollably.

His pale, ghostly face colored with the fiery heat of his anger. *I'm going to kill Norbrook first. I'm going to kill him so slowly and fill him with so much pain that he'll beg me for death.*

He made one final attempt to grab her again, but Lauren jumped away.

And slammed right into Colt's hard chest.

Only this time, it was the front of her that hit him. He was sitting up, facing her, grasping her shoulders so hard that his fingers hurt her. He gave her one final shake, and her eyes met his.

"What the hell were you dreaming, Lauren?"

His voice was harsh. And laced with—what? Fear? Concern? Lauren couldn't be sure.

Never mind what was in his voice. Never mind that he was holding her so close that her bare nipples were brushing lightly against the muscled hardness of his chest. Never mind the fact that she felt lost in his dark eyes. Never mind the fact that she was trembling in his arms.

She was alive.

Dillon hadn't been able to kill her so easily. Because Colt had woken her.

"He—he was going to kill me," she stammered, still out of breath.

"Who?"

"Dillon Waters—who else?" She probably would have been angry, but just then she didn't have the strength.

Colt looked around at the quiet cabin. "That's impossible."

"He was here," she insisted.

"All right, I'll go check." He got out of bed and moved away through the dark cabin, his footsteps silent. Lauren sat up and watched him. She held the sheet against her chest and could feel the rapid beating of her heart.

"There's no one here, Lauren," he said, quietly coming back to bed. "Only you and me. And everything is still locked up. It was just a dream. A bad one. A real bad one. But still just a dream." He was trying to convince her—and to put aside his own misgivings. Didn't his own grandfather and many other of his people put a great deal of faith in their dreams and visions? And hadn't his grandfather's last vision come true regarding Colt's destiny just as the old man had said it would? Colt fought to push the questions aside. This had to be a dream. There was no other explanation for it. Because Dillon could not have gotten in.

She saw disbelief in his eyes, and she fought the urge to slap him. Hard enough to give him the sense to believe her.

"I'm telling you he was here," she argued. Her growing anger gave her strength, putting power behind her words. "He tried to kill me!" She jumped out of bed, taking the sheet with her, and headed toward the bathroom.

"What are you doing?" he asked, following her, climbing out of bed a second time, seemingly not as concerned about his nudity as she was about hers.

She flipped on the bathroom light and was temporarily blinded by the sudden brightness. "Looking at my neck. There's bound to be some marks from his hands."

To her horror and surprise, there was nothing. No bruises. No redness. No prints from Dillon's fingers. Nothing.

She pulled her wild mass of red hair out of the way, and still she could see nothing. The pale flesh of her slender throat was flawless.

But the woman who stared back at her from the mirror looked wild, stormy, half crazed. Her hair was a mass of tangles, ringlets the color of fire falling in every direction. Her eyes were bright, eager, anxious, shining brighter than any emerald.

Had this wild look come from making love with Colt? Or was it from something more—from Dillon Waters trying to strangle her? Or had her experience with Dillon been just as Colt said, nothing but a dream?

Already the fear was fading. The dream was fading. Even the pain that had been in her throat was gone.

"I was so sure that he was here," she said slowly, her anger ebbing away, as well. "I could see him." She moved her hand to her cheek. "He touched me. He kissed me. It felt so cold, so horrible." Her eyes met Colt's in the mirror. He stood behind her.

Still holding her gaze, he leaned down and moved her hair aside before kissing her neck lightly.

"It was just a dream, Lauren," he repeated. "Come back to bed with me." His whisper was warm and seductive, and his lips brushed her neck with a slight tickle that sent hot trembling fires down her body.

She didn't want to go back to bed—at least not to sleep—but she did want the comfort of Colt's arms.

She remembered Dillon's words about Colt never being able to love her, and she tried to force them from her mind. She didn't care about love. Or did she? She closed her eyes tightly, trying to force all thoughts from her mind, trying to simply let her body feel Colt's touch, trying to erase the doubt.

At the same time, she remembered Colt's words. *Destiny be damned.*

She leaned down, turned on the faucet and splashed cold water on her face, trying to wash away the remnants of the dream.

Then she leaned back against Colt. His arms came around her, and he held her to him.

"What did you mean when you said destiny be damned?" she asked.

He tensed visibly, his eyes narrowing slightly. "Nothing," he replied quietly. "It was nothing. Don't worry about it." He worked again to force the image of his grandfather from his mind. He could still see the old man, in Native dress, looking worried. And after a moment, when he brought his lips to hers, he *was* able to forget. But that would never change his heritage. Nor would it change what his grandfather had told him about his destiny.

With one hand, he wiped the drops of water from her face. His gentle touch warmed her, soothed her. It didn't matter if what she'd experienced was a dream or not. She couldn't forget the fear. And only Colt's touch was strong enough to ease the terror. She let that touch take her to a place where there was nothing but pleasure and warmth. A safe place where there was only room for the two of them, a place where she needed to be....

Later, Colt held her in his arms, and Lauren rested her head on his chest, listening to the sounds of his breathing, mixed with the chirping of the morning birds outside.

The storm was long gone. It had eased away and faded into nothing, just as her dream of Dillon Waters had. A warm stream of sunshine etched its way across the wood floor of the cabin near the table. Lauren watched it, finding comfort in the sights and sounds of the morning, despite the idea that there was a crazed man waiting right outside to kill her. A crazed man who admitted to being dead, she reminded herself. She closed her eyes, wishing she didn't have to think about it, and tried to count the sure, strong beats of Colt's heart.

But with the coming of a new day, a new wave of fear was washing over her. Dillon Waters *was* out there, and he wanted her dead. Sooner or later, despite the chirping birds and the security offered by Colt's embrace, she was going to have to think about it. She was going to have to face it, in order to look for a way out.

"I'll be right back," Colt said, sliding out from under her.

"Where are you going?" She sat up and looked at him, suddenly afraid of being alone.

"Nature calls, Lauren." He gave her a quick kiss and a smile. "I'll be right back, I promise."

Lauren nearly shuddered at the thought of another promise—Dillon's. "Don't promise, okay?"

He gave her a puzzled look and absently slipped into his jeans, which he'd found on the floor beside the bed. "Okay," he agreed as he zipped his pants. He took her hand, giving it a squeeze.

Still holding her hand, he turned and headed toward the bathroom, letting go of her only when the distance between them grew too great. "Stay away from the windows, and don't look out."

Lauren sat in the middle of the bed, holding the sheet up to her chest. "All right." She watched him until the bathroom door closed, then took a deep breath. The question of what she should do came to her once again.

"Take it one moment at a time," she said out loud, not having any other answer. "Take whatever comes, and handle it as it happens. Sounds good, except now you're talking to yourself.

"I think I'm entitled," she added. "So what should I do at this moment?"

She looked around the large room, avoiding the windows. She spotted the coffeemaker on the counter. "Make a fresh pot of coffee," she replied to her own question. "Maybe even make some breakfast. It's so much easier to think on a full stomach."

She reached down beside the bed to get her clothes, and grabbed Colt's soft cotton shirt by mistake. She was about to set it aside and reach again when she paused.

She held his shirt up to her face and breathed in the heady scent of him. Without another thought, she slipped her arms into the sleeves and buttoned it up the front.

The floor was cool under her feet, but she ignored it, making her way to the counter, still avoiding the windows. She was pouring the old coffee from the night before down the drain when a new sound from outside touched her.

She listened to it for a long moment. It was the whining cry of a dog.

She set the pot on the counter and looked back at the bathroom door. It was still closed, and she could hear water running.

The cry seemed to be filling the entire cabin.

"Do you have a dog?" she called out to Colt.

Only the sound of running water came to her from the other side of the bathroom door.

What could one look hurt? she wondered. If she saw any sign of anything out of the ordinary, she'd turn her back. She'd keep her eyes down. It'd be fine.

Biting her lip, she moved to the back door and glanced out, quickly looking down.

What she saw stopped her in her tracks, and took away any thought of Dillon Waters or any other danger that might be lurking about.

Mav was out there.

Mav, her beautiful, faithful companion, who'd risked his life for her. He was just standing on the back step, looking up her. There was dried blood on his shoulder where Dillon Waters had stabbed him.

"Mav!" she gasped. "Oh, God, Mav!"

She didn't even question how he'd found her. She didn't care. All she cared about in that instant was that he was hurt and he needed her. She reached for the knob without thinking. He was looking up at her, his whining louder than ever. He was hurt. She had no choice but to help him.

She unlocked the door and turned the knob just as Colt came out of the bathroom. "Did you say something, Lauren?" he asked through the towel he was using to dry his face.

"It's just Mav," she explained, giving him nothing more than a quick glance.

"What?" He pulled the towel away to look at her. "Lauren! No!" he yelled to her from across the room. "What are you doing?"

Too late. The dog bounded in.

Lauren ignored Colt, her eyes riveted on Mav and the dried blood on his coat. "It's all right, Mav. We'll help you. It's all right." She cooed to him as though he were a hurt child.

But the dog wasn't looking at her. He was looking at Colt. He bared his teeth and snarled. The sound was loud and harsh in the quiet cabin. He stalked toward Colt without fear or hesitation. His growl continued, deepening in intensity.

"Mav, sit!" Lauren commanded. She understood that the dog was injured and might not be thinking rationally. She'd had him at the inn for over three years, and she'd never before heard him growl at a human being.

The animal ignored her, stalking across the room toward Colt.

"Mav, I said sit. Now!"

He didn't even respond to the sound of her voice, much less the command.

"Lauren," Colt said evenly, never taking his eyes from the dog. "Shut the door and lock it."

Lauren was staring at Mav, unable to believe that the dog was stalking Colt in such a way and ignoring her. Suddenly he didn't look like her dog at all.

"Lauren, shut the damned door!"

Lauren obeyed this time, shutting the door and locking it just as the animal leapt at Colt.

Lauren screamed. Mav landed on Colt, and Colt seemed to be ready for it, for the force and weight of the dog didn't knock him off his feet. He tried to use the towel he held as a barrier between Mav's teeth and his body.

For a moment, Colt appeared to be dancing with the huge dog in his arms. And Lauren stood frozen in terror, one hand over her mouth, stifling another scream.

Colt held the dog by its neck, huge tufts of Mav's thick fur bunched in his fists. He was holding the dog away from him, trying to keep him from reaching his throat. But all the dog could seem to get, fortunately, was mouthfuls of the towel Colt still held.

"My gun, Lauren—" Colt ground out the words. "Shoot him."

Lauren couldn't seem to react. All she was able to do was stare.

The weight and force of the large dog was suddenly too much for Colt, and he lost his balance and crashed into one of the nearby kitchen chairs. He lost his grip on the dog with one hand, and Mav sank his teeth into Colt's bare shoulder.

"Lauren!"

The sight of Mav biting Colt, and the sight of Colt's blood, would have been enough to get Lauren moving. But it was the harsh cry that came from Colt's lips that sent shivers of panic through her and seemed to get her adrenaline pumping. She scrambled toward the night table, moving in a roundabout way to avoid the man and the animal.

She grabbed Colt's gun with both hands, trying desperately to keep the barrel from shaking, turned and pointed it at Mav. And pulled the trigger.

Nothing happened.

CHAPTER SIX

Lauren let out a frustrated cry. "It doesn't work!" She turned the gun in her hands, looking at it closely, careful not to point it toward her own face. Oh, God, had Dillon Waters done something to Colt's gun?

Colt and Mav were still on the floor, a raging mass of man and growling beast. Mav was wild, attacking Colt with everything he had. And Colt, likewise, was using everything he had to defend himself. He let go of the dog with one hand and punched him, right in the face. The force of the blow sent the dog reeling, but it was mere seconds before he was leaping back again in a full-force attack.

And Lauren couldn't get the damned gun to fire.

"The safety—" Colt bit out.

She flipped the safety and pointed the gun back at Mav. Then what she was about to do hit her. She stared at them, hesitating long enough that Mav was able to bite Colt again, this time on his muscled forearm.

"I'm sorry, Mav," she whispered, tears instantly coming to her eyes.

She pulled the trigger, and the crack of the gun going off echoed through the cabin with a deafening roar. The impact of the bullet knocked Mav off Colt and into a corner by the fireplace, where he fell in a lifeless heap. The loud growling stopped in an instant, and the room was suddenly quiet. Quiet as death.

Lauren stood there, still holding the gun, wondering if the dog was going to come back to life, just as Dillon Waters had. The only sound in the room was the harsh sound of Lauren's rapid breathing. Tears were streaming down her cheeks, but she ignored them. She stared at the dog. Now, in death, the animal looked more like the Mav she knew and loved. Her dog, her friend. Slowly, very slowly, she sank to her knees, no longer able to stand up.

Colt dragged himself to his feet and made his way over to her.

Tenderly he took the gun from her hands. "Lauren?"

She looked up at him, finally, but his image was blurred by her tears. Blood seeped from the bites on his shoulder and his arm. His face was filled with pain, yet his eyes held a tenderness that melted her heart.

He cocked the safety on the gun and placed the weapon down the top of his jeans. Pulling her to her feet, he righted the chair he'd knocked over during his fight with Mav and helped her into it.

"Do you think he's going to come back to life like Dillon Waters did?" she asked, her voice sounding hollow.

"I don't think so, but let's wait a minute and see." Colt didn't believe for one minute that the dog was going to come back to life, but then, he was still having trouble comprehending the fact that Dillon Waters had. So he waited.

When nothing happened, he left Lauren on the chair and hesitantly moved toward the still body of the dog. He pulled out his gun again and held it ready before reaching out to grab Mav. Then, slowly, he grasped the end of the dog's tail and dragged him toward the back door.

"What are you doing?" Lauren gasped, rising to her feet.

"I'm going to put him outside, under the deck."

"No!" She took a step to the left, putting herself between Colt and the door.

"Why not?" he questioned.

"You are not opening that door," she replied, emphasizing each word. "It might give something else the chance to come in here and attack us."

Colt stared at her. "He didn't attack us, Red, he attacked me."

"Well, then we're not letting anything else in here to attack *you*."

He let go of Mav's tail. "What do you suggest I do with him, then? I'm not going to just leave him here in the middle of the kitchen."

There was a long moment of silence before Lauren replied. "Don't you have a closet or something, just somewhere we could put him until this is over and we can bury him?"

It was Colt's turn to be silent. Then he let out a sigh. "There's a closet in the bathroom. I could put him in there."

Lauren nodded, her throat still tight with emotion. The idea that Mav really was dead, and that she had shot him, was finally, slowly, beginning to sink in. She sank down again on the chair she'd sat on before and watched Colt pick up Mav's tail once again and drag him toward the bathroom.

Once they were out of Lauren's vision, she didn't bother to move so that she could see more. She just sat still, her heart breaking, piece by piece. Icy fear was pulsing through her veins like cold slivers of steel. The inn would never be the same without Mav. And at the same time, Lauren couldn't forget the horrible sound of his growling. The dog she had loved and the dog that had attacked Colt were not one and the same.

She heard the thud of the closing of the closet in the bathroom and looked up to see Colt returning. There was more blood trickling down his arm.

She stood up, forcing her shaking legs to obey her and keep her on her feet. Absently she wiped away the tears that streaked her cheeks. "Sit down," she said. "I'll take care of your arm."

Colt's eyes met hers from across the room, and for a long moment Lauren thought he was going to refuse her. Finally he came over and sat down on the chair she'd just vacated. The antiseptic and gauze were still sitting on the kitchen table where Colt had left them the night before, and Lauren reached for them now.

The room was quiet, and Colt never moved as Lauren cleaned the bites and bandaged them.

His tanned skin was smooth and warm beneath her fingers, and her heart quickened its pace when she touched him. She had to force herself to concentrate on cleaning his wounds to keep from sliding her hands down his chest. It took everything she had not to throw herself in his arms. He was perfect, like some bronze statue, and she thought she would never tire of touching him. He was the vision of an Indian warrior sitting tall and proud atop a great black stallion.

Like the brave in her thoughts, he sat still and quiet the entire time it took for her to tend to him. And touching him worked wonders when it came to calming her fears.

"How's your hand feel?" he asked.

"A little tight, but not too bad." After making love with Colt, experiencing the dream of Dillon Waters and having to shoot Mav, she'd completely forgotten her injured hand. The cut on her palm now seemed so petty. "There," she said, finishing up. "How's that feel?"

"Great," he muttered. "What about your shoulder?"

"It's fine," she answered honestly, moving around to face him and sit in the chair next to him. She was relishing how good it felt to be thinking of something other than Dillon Waters trying to kill her, even if it was Colt's state of health. "When's the last time you had a tetanus shot?"

"I don't know," he replied. "I take it that Mav had his shots?"

"Yes, every year," she replied, fighting against the tightness of her throat.

Lauren crossed her arms and hugged herself, still feeling cold. "I don't understand why he attacked you. Mav's never hurt anyone. He was so used to strangers at the inn."

"He was hurt, Lauren. Any hurt or sick animal is bound to be unpredictable."

She shook her head slowly. "No, I don't believe that."

"Well, what do you believe?" He reached out a tender hand and rested it on her leg.

She was going to cry again if she didn't get a grip on her emotions. "I don't know. I think Dillon Waters had something to do with what Mav did. My dog wouldn't have attacked without a reason."

The fact that Colt didn't appear surprised by her words told her he'd already thought the same thing. She reached out and took his hand. There was something more, she thought. Something that she should remember, but couldn't. Was it something Dillon Waters had said to her or something Colt had mentioned? She couldn't be sure, she just knew there were missing pieces, pieces that might explain why Mav had attacked Colt.

"How is he doing this?" she asked slowly. "How could he control me like he did, and now possibly Mav? Just what is he?"

Colt's eyes held hers. "I don't know," he replied honestly. "But I intend to find out."

"What are we going to do?"

Colt flexed his arm, testing the tightness of the bandage Lauren had put on. "First we're going to get something to eat."

"I don't think I can eat," Lauren said. Her stomach was filled with a sick feeling of cold terror, and she didn't think she could keep anything down.

"Yes, you can, and you will," Colt replied. "Dillon Waters already has us at too much of a disadvantage. From now on, we've got to be at our best if we're going to have any hope at all of getting through this."

Lauren couldn't argue with that, but she still knew she was going to have to work to keep anything he fed her in its rightful place. "All right," she finally agreed. "What then?" She wanted to think about the future. She wanted to think she had a future.

"We're getting out of here."

That was the last thing she would have expected to hear him say. "You can't be serious. I'm not setting one foot outside this cabin. You've seen what can happen...." She knew she was babbling, and still she couldn't stop. The thought of what could happen overwhelmed her. Inside the cabin, with the doors locked, she was safe, wasn't she? He'd convinced her of that.

Now he was telling her he'd changed his mind and was sending her outside. He might as well be sending her into a den of lions.

His grip on her hand tightened. "Lauren," he said softly, in an attempt to bring her rising hysteria under control, "we can't stay here forever."

"Why not?" she asked. She knew there were reasons, she just wanted to hear him say what they were.

"Because if we're ever going to find a way to stop Waters, we've got to go out there and hunt for it." His heated gaze held hers. "He's not about to bring it to us while he's delivering a pizza."

Lauren bit her lip, not caring right then if she ever beat that old habit or not. "I'm afraid," she confessed.

"So am I," he replied softly.

Lauren gave him a small smile, surprised at his confession, but feeling closer to him because he trusted her enough to tell her. Then she grew serious. "If he can control me as much as he does from out there, what do you think he'll be able to do if there are no walls between us?"

Tenderness and the courage of his heritage burned in the depths of Colt's eyes. "It's a chance we'll have to take. If we're lucky, maybe the walls don't have anything to do with how much he's able to control you. Maybe his hold on you won't grow any stronger."

Still biting her lip, she looked down so that he couldn't see that she lacked his courage. "Where will we go?" she asked softly. "Where do we start?"

"With his father," he replied, just as softly.

Lauren's eyes widened in surprise. "Dillon Waters's father? Do you know him?"

"He lives about thirty miles north of here, on the other side of the lake."

Lauren stared at him now, her curiosity stronger than her fear. "How did you know that?"

It was Colt's turn to look away. "After Dillon Waters was shot," he said slowly, "I took care of the paperwork that was necessary to have him flown home for burial. That's how I knew he originally came from this area. And—" his words grew even slower "—I guess there's just some things you never forget.

"Listen, why don't I fix some breakfast?" he said, changing the subject. "I'm not much of a cook, but I haven't starved yet." He flashed her a grin, and his lighter mood added some much-needed brightness to the room.

Lauren didn't reply, didn't return his grin. She simply stared at him as pieces of the puzzle began falling into place. "You took care of the paperwork," she echoed slowly. "Then you were involved in the shooting, weren't you?"

He was quiet for a long moment, his expression flat and hard. "It was my task force, my team, that was in charge of bringing him out."

Lauren couldn't tear her gaze from his, watching as his eyes darkened, growing hooded to the point that she couldn't tell anything at all as to what he might be feeling. Then he turned away altogether, getting up from his chair and moving to a nearby cabinet to retrieve a skillet. "Now, how about some breakfast?" he asked.

Lauren knew that was the end of the conversation for the time being, and that any other questions she might have would have to wait until he was ready to answer them. "Okay. I need to wash up and get dressed," she replied, trying to lighten her tone, but finding it difficult. She grasped the top button of the shirt she wore and tugged gently, lifting it away from her before releasing it. "Can I keep this?" she asked slowly. He turned back slightly to see what she was asking, and her eyes met his hesitantly. She was still grasping his shirt. It seemed an oddly intimate question. She let go of the soft cotton fabric and ran her hand down the front of the shirt, the warmth of it reminding her of his touch. The gentle scent of it was solely his.

His eyes softened. "Sure," he replied.

Lauren looked toward the bathroom. "I'm also going to leave the door open," she said softly, knowing Colt was going to think she'd finally lost it and gone completely crazy. But Mav was in there. And it didn't matter that the dog was locked in a closet. Lauren didn't want to be shut up in there with the dead animal.

Colt seemed to understand this. "Good idea," he muttered before placing the skillet on the stove.

Lauren watched him for another moment as he moved to the sink and continued the job she'd started of fixing a fresh pot of coffee. Then she headed toward the bathroom.

Once inside the small room, she paused to stare at the closet door. For one brief moment, she contemplated opening that door just enough to see Mav. She had the strangest feeling that he was alive in there and was just waiting for the chance to pounce on her. She drew close enough to the door to press her ear against it, but silence was all that touched her. There was no growling, no panting. And, much to her relief, no voice making any commands.

She forced herself to move away from the door and run water in the sink, water that was cold enough to sting her face when she splashed it on her skin. She heard something frying in the kitchen as she patted her face dry, and the appetizing aromas of bacon and brewing coffee touched her senses. Well, maybe she was hungry after all. Eating would probably make her feel better, she thought.

Then she looked up at her reflection in the mirror. Oh, God, she thought, it was going to take a hell of a lot more than food and a hot cup of coffee to make the woman in the mirror look anything like the way Lauren remembered herself.

Her red hair was in wild array, appearing as if she'd stuck her finger in an electrical outlet. Her face was pale. No, more than pale. It held more of a chalky gray tone. And, to complete the picture, there were dark, puffy purple circles under her eyes. Lauren could remember looking better after her worst bouts with the flu.

And with no makeup available, there was little she could do about it. She didn't even have a hairbrush. There was a small comb on the vanity, but, knowing it would never get through the tangles, Lauren didn't even reach for it.

What must Colt think of her? Not only did she look like hell, but she'd jumped into bed with him, not once but *twice*. And she'd done it with very little thought as to how she would feel afterward.

After finishing her business, Lauren walked back into the main room and saw that Colt was standing at the stove. His back was to her, but she could see him turning a long slice of bacon. Just then, two pieces of toast popped up out of the toaster on the counter near him.

Moving to the bed, she sat on the edge, and had put one leg in her jeans when she froze, amazed at how normal everything in the room appeared. It seemed like a typical morning. Sunlight was pouring in through the windows. The appealing aroma of breakfast was heavy in the air. The table was set and waiting.

Normal?

Not by a long shot. Somewhere out there was a maniac who wanted to kill her, who had the ability to put thoughts into her head and send her own dog in to attack another human being. And if that wasn't enough, she'd spent the night doing something she thought she'd never in her life do. She'd had sex with a man she barely knew.

A mystery man. A man who brought her more questions than answers. And yet, with each question, she felt more drawn to him.

Who was Colt Norbrook, really? And how did he feel about her?

She stared at his smooth, tanned back. Unaware she was watching him, he continued cooking, the muscles in his back rippling with his movements. God, what had she done? She didn't even know him. So how was his touch able to erase any will she had to refuse him?

"What's the matter, Lauren?" he asked.

The sound of his voice was enough to shock her out of her study of him, but his question left her wondering if perhaps he had eyes in the back of his head.

"Nothing," she replied, a little too quickly. "Why?"

He turned and gave her an intense look. "Just checking," he replied. "You've been sitting there for nearly three whole minutes without moving."

It was a polite way of telling her he knew she'd been staring at him. "I was just thinking," she said.

He turned back to the skillet of bacon and didn't question her further. Lauren had the feeling he didn't need to ask, because he already knew what—and who—she'd been thinking about.

"Do you want your eggs scrambled or fried?" he asked.

"Scrambled," she replied.

So this was what the morning after a one-night stand was like, she thought, finally sliding her other leg into her jeans and pulling them up. Two people who have just been as close as they can possibly get suddenly stand apart and avoid each other. Steering clear of any conversation that might draw them closer or expose their feelings. Instead, they talk about eggs. She supposed the weather would be their next topic.

"Could you pour the coffee?" he asked, indicating with a jerk of his head the coffeepot that had been placed on the table.

"Sure," she replied, thinking she'd been wrong. Their next topic hadn't been the weather. Well, they still had time to get to it.

She secured his shirt by tying it at her waist, then took the pot and poured coffee into two waiting cups. Looking at the table closer, she was surprised to see the pattern on his dishes.

"Flowers?" she questioned, wondering if he'd chosen the pattern himself. Picking up a plate, she held it out toward him as he turned around to see what she meant.

"Yeah," he replied, turning back to the stove, where he began removing the bacon from the skillet.

"If you don't mind my saying so, these don't look like something a man would pick out," she said.

"They weren't."

Well, she'd asked for it. A woman had picked these out for him. But who? Someone he'd once lived with? Maybe even an ex-wife?

"My mother," he added suddenly, stopping any further mental questions. "She said I might have company someday. And I guess this is someday. I don't get company too often, especially for breakfast, so I thought we'd use the real thing and not my usual paper."

"Oh" was all Lauren could think to reply. So what if his mother had picked out the dishes. That still didn't answer the question of a past live-in, or an ex-wife.

Why was she pondering these questions, anyway? She should be thinking of a way to keep Dillon Waters from killing her. Besides, it wasn't as if Colt were asking to move in with her.

She almost wished he'd stuck with eating on paper plates. Seeing the table set so prettily and thinking of Dillon Waters was a somewhat frightening combination. She felt as though this were her last meal, and Colt was trying to make it nice by serving it on china.

And something else kept nagging at her. There was something about her dream last night that she wanted— needed—to remember.

She took a sip of her coffee and tried to piece together her fragmented memories of last night's terror. Now, in the daylight, it did seem like nothing more than a dream. And, as with a dream, so much of it had faded. She could remember Dillon Waters caressing her cheek. She could remember feeling him choking her. And had he kissed her or tried to kiss her? Lauren wasn't sure. She tried to recall what he'd said to her— something about loving him.

But she just couldn't remember his words. Nor could she remember ever loving him. She didn't even know him.

She glanced back at Colt, who was now stirring the eggs. Not knowing *him* hadn't stopped her from going to bed with him. She absently bit her lip and rubbed the bridge of her nose, feeling the first pangs of a coming headache.

"You'll probably feel better after you have something to eat," said Colt.

Again his voice and words startled her, and she turned to find him watching her.

"Maybe," she muttered. She set her cup down, finding her hand shaking slightly.

"Could you grab the plate of bacon and the toast, and I'll dish out the eggs?"

"Of course," she replied, moving to the counter. They passed one another. It was the closest they had been all morning, after spending the night with no space between them.

She set the bacon and toast on the table, and the two of them sat down.

Lauren stared squarely at Colt as more pieces of her memory fell into place. With the intensity of a bolt of lightning, she suddenly recalled just what it was that she hadn't remembered before.

And the realization almost scared her to death.

CHAPTER SEVEN

"Dillon Waters did have something to do with Mav attacking you," she told Colt slowly. The thoughts were coming to her as though they had to pass through a thick fog to reach her. "He said he was going to kill you first. He was so angry at you for taking me away from him."

Colt returned her intense look. "When did he tell you this? Yesterday, when I took you away from your inn? And just when did he have the chance to have any serious conversation with you?"

She shook her head. Her headache growing, she told him everything she could remember. About how angry Dillon had been, about the things he'd said.

"He growled—no, it was more like a howl, like an animal." Then she realized just how Dillon Waters had sounded. "He sounded just like Mav when he attacked you."

"Lauren, we've already talked about this. The dog was hurt. And Dillon Waters never howled. He never even really talked to you. It was just a dream."

Why couldn't she make him understand? Why couldn't he see or hear what she could?

"I'm telling you, it was no dream," she insisted, trying to control her voice. "I was awake. When I opened my eyes, I could see the log wall of the cabin in front of me. And when I closed them I could see Dillon Waters.

He was really here. He spoke to me. He touched me. I could feel him the entire time."

"Lauren..." Colt said, speaking her name as though she were an unruly child and he was forced to muster every ounce of his patience before going on. "You're reading more into this than what's really here. I've seen it a million times through my police work. You're terrified. I understand that. Knowing Waters wants to kill you, you have every right to be. You're beginning to see him in everything else around you."

Lauren stared at him from across the table. He was writing her off as some overemotional woman, and her anger at him was growing faster than her passion had last night.

"But look at the facts," he went on. "Number one, the cabin was, and still is, locked up tighter than a drum. Waters couldn't have gotten in without us knowing about it. Number two, you were dreaming. Seeing the log wall was just part of the dream, because I had to shake you—quite a bit, I might add—in order to wake you up. Number three, that dog was hurt. I could see that, and so could you. And no animal acts rationally or predictably when it's hurt." He paused, and reached over to cover her hand with his.

"Those are the facts, pure and simple. You're not just letting your imagination run wild, you're mixing it with all the fear you're experiencing," he finished.

Oh, great, she thought sarcastically. Not only was he labeling her as overemotional, but he'd added over-imaginative to the growing list of her faults. Any moment, she knew, he was going to go on to explain that there were no ghosts in the closet or monsters under the bed.

"But I heard his voice. It was so clear, so close," she told him.

"Do you hear it now?" he asked.

"No."

"Have you heard it at all this morning?" His eyes never left hers.

"No," she said again.

The room was quiet for a moment. "It was just part of the dream, Lauren."

"But it wasn't!" she argued, her voice rising. "You're not talking about just anybody. You're talking about a man who's supposed to be dead!"

Following her outburst, the room grew quiet again. Lauren looked down at her plate, but she could still feel Colt's eyes on her.

"Let's try to take one thing at a time," he said gently, sounding as though he didn't know what else to say. "Okay?"

His voice, with its evident gentleness mixed with firm strength, was almost enough to make her believe any words he might utter. Maybe it was as he said—she was simply letting her imagination run wild. Perhaps all her fears *were* caused by Dillon Waters's attempts on her life. It would seem only natural that her subconscious would manifest her terror in the form of a dream. And as for Mav, he'd been hurt. That was why she'd let him in. Perhaps he'd recognized her, but seen Colt as a threat. Still, it all sounded too easy, too simple.

"I don't know if I can take it one thing at a time. With every occurrence, there's more fear. Besides, you're making this all sound so logical, and you're the one who first said Dillon Waters was dead. If he's really dead, then how the hell is he doing any of this?

Unless, of course, he isn't dead. In which case, you were wrong. You could be wrong about everything.''

"Maybe I am wrong. The truth is, I have no hard answers. And until I get some, I'm going to concentrate on doing whatever it takes to keep him from getting his hands on you.''

"Us.''

"All right, us,'' he muttered. "Let's leave this for now, okay? Eat your breakfast before it gets cold.''

She tried to comply, but the eggs tasted like rubber and the toast like sawdust. Even the coffee didn't seem hot enough, and the bacon was far from appetizing. Lauren felt lucky to get down a bite of everything.

She watched Colt with wide eyes. He apparently enjoyed his own cooking, and cleaned his plate with gusto.

"Do you have any aspirin?'' she asked, feeling her headache growing.

He retrieved a bottle from the bathroom and set it on the table next to her plate before moving to find a shirt. Lauren took two of the tablets and forced them down with a drink of her coffee.

Then she cleared the table, putting everything into the sink, while Colt finished dressing. The Western shirt of red and turquoise that he now wore made his Native American heritage more prominent than ever.

Lauren followed him as he walked to the other side of the fireplace into the living room area. Against the wall was a gun cabinet she hadn't noticed before.

Colt unlocked it and began removing the guns, one by one. He took out a rifle and another handgun, checking each before placing them gently on the sofa.

"That's quite an arsenal,'' she commented, looking at all the weapons he'd left in the cabinet. "I take it you're not against gun control.''

He grinned at her. "Oh, no, I'm all for gun control. I believe anyone who holds a gun should have complete control over it." He loaded the handgun. "Do you think you can have control over this one?"

He held the gun out to her.

"I fired your other one twice," she noted.

"True. This one fires nearly the same. So I'm sure you can do it. What I'm asking you is if you feel you have enough control to keep it with you and use it if necessary. When you fired the gun before, you were reacting on instinct. Tell me, do you even remember pulling the trigger yesterday, when you shot Waters?" he asked.

Lauren looked down at the gun in Colt's hands, then moved her eyes upward till she met his dark gaze. "No," she replied finally. She could hardly remember grabbing the gun off the floor, much less using it on Dillon Waters. What seemed to stand out in her mind more than anything was the way the bullets had slammed into his body, hitting him with enough force to knock him away from her. She also recalled vividly her horror at not seeing any blood, only the holes in his shirt.

"I didn't think so," Colt said softly. "If I give this to you, it will be your decision when to draw it. And if you do draw it, you must do so with every intention of using it," he said, emphasizing the word *using*. "You can't use it simply to scare someone off. You don't pull it out unless you have complete control and feel you can fire it. Otherwise, Red, it could be turned against you. Do you think you can handle it?"

The way he called her Red reminded her of the passion with which he'd made love to her. It reminded her of the soft ways he'd touched her and the gentle words he'd spoken to her.

She swallowed hard, wishing she knew the answer to his question. "What if I can't?" she asked.

He shrugged slightly. "My gun was available when you needed to grab it both times. And you were able to use it then. If Dillon Waters is coming at you, I want you to be able to protect yourself. I don't want you to have to depend on me to save you."

And that was her problem. She did depend on him. And she wanted to continue depending on him. She wanted him to be there for her, like that Indian brave riding in to rescue her. She'd stood on her own two feet for too long. Forever, it seemed. Especially since the first accident. How many times since then had she wished there was someone there with her? Someone strong, who would take her in his arms and tell her everything was going to be fine. That she wasn't alone.

No one knew that after that terrifying ride home when her truck's brakes went out she'd come home and hugged Mav, simply because there was no one else.

Colt's words confused her. What was he saying, anyway? He didn't want her to depend on him? Was that his way of telling her that last night had been nothing more than a one-night stand, and that after Dillon Waters was no longer a threat Colt would be out of her life? *Destiny be damned,* he had said before he made love to her. The man made no sense. In some ways he was more of a mystery than Dillon Waters. Just what the hell did he want from her, anyway?

Colt Norbrook had surely gotten what he'd wanted, she thought with sudden despair. He'd kissed her once, and that was all it had taken for her to fall into bed with him.

God, how could she have been such a fool?

And through all of her contemplation, he continued to stand there, looking at her with his black, depthless eyes—waiting for her answer.

"Do you think you can handle carrying this?" he asked again.

She was suddenly filled with new purpose, new determination. It felt good. She felt the way she had when she first opened the inn, when she had known she was in full charge of something good. She might not have control over Dillon Waters, but at least the gun would give her some control over what he might try to do to her.

Of course, a gun wouldn't give her any control over Colt or how he'd respond to her after all this was over. However, she did have control over herself, and how she reacted to him and to his touch. She was determined not to let Colt hurt her. She could enjoy good sex just as well as he could. That didn't mean she had to let him near her heart. Right? Yet the way he was looking at her made her suddenly unsure. Last night she had felt as if she and Colt were communicating in a way she'd never communicated with another man before. They had told one another more without the use of words than Lauren would ever have thought possible. And they had done it together, hadn't they? Had it been the same for him?

She reached out and took the gun from him. "I can handle it," she said. Yes, she thought with a new wave of confidence, she could handle anything. Dillon Waters had been so confident that he would kill her. Well, she could be just as confident that she wouldn't let him.

The gun was cool in her hand. She looked down at it, feeling the weight of it.

"I've got a shoulder holster for it," Colt said.

"Great," she muttered. She was feeling more and more like the confident woman who'd handled the gas leak at the inn with such expertise. And the woman who'd controlled the truck with no brakes. What did it matter that she'd felt as though she might be falling apart after both episodes had ended. She had handled them fine while they were happening.

She almost smiled.

Then she glanced up at Colt. His expression caused her to freeze, and kept her smile from reaching her lips. He was alert again, on guard, looking over her shoulder toward the kitchen area.

"What is it?" she asked softly.

"I heard something outside. On the deck."

"What?" she asked. It was amazing just how quickly terror could fill her again, shattering the confidence she'd been so proud of only moments before.

"I don't know." He picked up the rifle on the sofa and quickly loaded it. "Stay here," he ordered, leaving her to stand in the middle of the room.

Lauren's heart raced as he crept toward the kitchen door. She glanced down at the gun in her hand. Was she going to have to use it so soon? Would she even be able to? Confident or not, she hoped she'd never have to make the decision. Her gaze was drawn back to Colt. He reached the back door and peered out.

She clamped her mouth shut to keep from warning him not to get too close to the glass, that something might leap through it. Then she felt like laughing. Her imagination really was running wild.

Colt looked out the window and chuckled, putting the gun down and relaxing visibly. "It's just an old gray cat who comes around sometimes."

"It's not injured like Mav was, is it?" Lauren asked, stepping around the fireplace and into the kitchen.

"No," he replied. He turned toward her. "Relax, Lauren. Not every animal is out to attack us."

It was another simple statement. So why didn't she believe it?

"Ready to go?" he asked.

No, she wasn't, and she knew that she never would be. She imagined it was a little like having the executioner ask you if you were ready right before he put the noose around your neck.

"I guess," she lied.

He helped her with the shoulder holster. "Check that out," he instructed, "and see how easy it is for you to reach the handle of the gun."

Lauren drew the weapon. "It feels fine." At least she thought it felt all right. How was she supposed to know? She'd never fired a gun until yesterday.

Her heart was hammering in her chest at the thought of leaving the safety of the cabin. Then his eyes met hers, and her heart hammered faster. God, why did he have to look at her in that way and make her feel as though she had all the courage in the world when she knew she didn't? Worse, why did he have to look at her the same way he'd looked at her before he'd kissed her last night—as though he had feelings for her. That one look was enough to send warm tingles through her.

She took a deep breath and tried to collect all her out-of-control emotions.

There was nothing left for them to do but leave.

He took her hand. "We'll go slow and keep our eyes open. The last thing we want to do is run out there and bump into him. Right?"

His voice was calm, but his words brought no comfort. Slow or fast, they could still run into Dillon Waters. He could still be waiting just around the corner. Yet, Lauren nodded her agreement.

He reached again for the rifle.

Hand in hand, they moved to the door. He let go of her to open the door. His hand on the knob, Colt paused and turned to her again. He looked into her eyes, his expression tender. He gave her a small smile. Letting go of the doorknob, he brought his hand to her face, cupping the softness of her cheek with his palm.

"Whatever happens, Red . . ." He didn't go on, but Lauren understood. He simply had no words to say, just as Lauren had no reply. His eyes filled with tenderness, he leaned down and touched his lips gently to hers.

That simple touch, that simple action, said so much more than any words could have. It told her he'd be there with her, no matter what. He'd be there with her to the end, if it came to that. She wished it could be forever.

But Lauren couldn't ask for forever. She couldn't ask for words of love or promises of tomorrow. For no words could express the importance of the commitment she felt he was making to her with that single touch of his lips.

And she wished it would never end. She wished time could stand still, preserving that kiss forever. But it couldn't, and he pulled away long before she was ready to let him go.

Slowly, he turned the knob and opened the door. Then he took her hand again.

Lauren expected all sorts of things to happen. An old gray cat sat perched on the rail of the deck, watching them. Lauren expected it to pounce on them. It didn't.

It merely stared at them for a moment before beginning its morning bath.

She expected Dillon Waters to jump out from behind every tree in front of them. But, to her surprise, nothing happened. They made their way around the cabin to Colt's motorcycle where they stood for a moment while Colt looked around. When he was convinced nothing would happen and no one was around, he slipped the rifle into a pouch on the cycle. Silently he handed her the only helmet, then pulled on his dark glasses. Then he climbed on, and at his silent invitation, Lauren climbed on behind him and clasped her hands around his muscled waist.

He started the bike, the roar of the engine sounding incredibly loud in the morning quiet. Colt turned his head slightly back toward her. "You all right?" he asked.

His concern touched her like the warm rays of the morning sun, and she nodded. "Do you think he's watching, that he's close?" Lauren asked, speaking into his ear.

He turned even more toward her, offering her his strong, proud profile. "I don't see any sign of him around," he muttered.

Lauren breathed easier. "Good," she said softly. "As long as I don't hear his voice anymore, I think I'll be fine."

She heard a chuckle just as the words left her mouth. She gasped, turning, thinking Dillon Waters stood just behind her.

"What?" Colt was just about to get them moving when her gasp stopped him.

"I thought I heard something," she said. Colt was bound to think she was crazy if she told him she'd heard laughing.

"It's just the lake rippling in the breeze," said Colt.

"Probably," she said, not at all convinced. She tried to smile and tightened her grip on Colt's waist.

But as they pulled away from the cabin, she could have sworn she heard Dillon Waters's laughter echoing in the wind.

CHAPTER EIGHT

Lauren's second ride on Colt's motorcycle was very different from her first.

This time, Lauren was wide-awake and able to see where Colt was taking her. She noticed everything, looking for any sign of Dillon Waters. She watched the drivers and passengers of cars that passed them, searching for any resemblance. She half expected to see him standing on the side of the road, waiting to jump out in front of them. The highway followed the edge of the lake, and Lauren even watched the boats on the water, looking for any sign of him.

She was also more aware of Colt this trip. He was no longer just a man in front of her that she could lean on. He was the man who was helping her—her support. He was the man who had taken her to the edge of the earth the night before, when he made love to her. He was her reality in a world that had suddenly grown utterly unpredictable.

He was looking around, too, searching for anything out of the ordinary. Looking for Dillon Waters.

Worry and anxiety were getting the best of Lauren. She was almost beginning to wish Dillon Waters would just show himself so that they could get the confrontation over with. She thought of all the things she wanted to say to him. Like calling him a coward for not meeting her face-to-face.

They had reached an area outside Rock Hill, a place known as the bottom land. It was a poorer section of town, near the edge of the lake, and usually only seen by tourists if they became lost. Most of the area tended to flood when the rains grew too heavy in the spring. The majority of its residents lived in run-down, half-washed-out homes and trailers. And according to Colt, Dillon Waters's father lived here.

Colt steered the motorcycle to Griff Waters's trailer and killed the vehicle's engine.

Lauren got off the cycle apprehensively. A musty dampness hung heavy in the air. There were a number of rusting, abandoned automobiles nearby. She took note of an old manual plow that looked as though it hadn't moved in decades. There were several old sheds that caused her to wonder just how they remained standing, and Lauren was easily able to convince herself that Dillon was hiding out in one of them.

Hiding. And watching. Always watching.

Colt climbed off the motorcycle, and his gaze combed the area.

The entire place seemed to have grown still at their arrival.

Lauren listened for a long moment to the silence. "He's here," she whispered. "He's close."

Colt halted his inspection to meet her gaze. "How do you know?" he asked softly.

She looked at him, hoping he couldn't readily see the fear she was feeling. "Just before he tried to kill me at the inn, everything grew silent, just like it is now. There weren't any birds chirping. No crickets. The breeze wasn't even blowing. Everything was so still." Still as death, she thought.

Colt's gaze left hers again to take in the area. He slipped the rifle from the pouch. "Well, if he is, he could be hiding anywhere."

Gee, that's a comfort, Lauren thought.

He turned away. "Come on," he said, his voice still soft. "Let's get this over with, so we can get out of here." He took her hand and gave it a gentle squeeze.

"That sounds like the best idea I've heard all morning," she replied.

Slowly, both of them looking around constantly, they approached Griff Waters's small, neglected trailer. The only sound was that of their footfalls on the loose gravel of the driveway.

Lauren didn't want to go up those three steps to the trailer door. She was terrified of who or what waited them just on the other side. She had the horrid feeling that Dillon Waters stood there, smiling as he watched her come closer and closer. Despite the warmth of the sunshine, she shivered.

They reached the steps, and Colt reluctantly let go of her hand to step up the first one. Just then, the door swung open.

The suddenness of it caused Lauren to jump back with a gasp. But Colt was ready, and the opening of the door was enough to cause him to raise the rifle.

The man who stood in the doorway glared at them.

Lauren stared at him. "My God..." she muttered.

Here was an older version of Dillon Waters. He took in the rifle Colt held, and his glare quickly became a scowl.

"Who the hell are you?" the man snapped. "And how dare you bring a gun onto my property!"

Colt lowered the rifle slightly, but still held it at the ready. "Are you Griff Waters?" he asked.

Lauren wanted to laugh at the question, thinking she didn't need to hear the answer. She already knew.

"Are you going to shoot me if I am?"

"No. Not without good reason," Colt added.

"Yeah," the man replied in a gruff, hard voice. "I'm Griff Waters. All my friends call me Griff. Who the hell are you?" he asked again. He looked hard at Colt, deliberately ignoring the rifle. Lauren couldn't tell if he was unafraid or just very good at hiding his fear.

"Colt Norbrook, and this is Lauren Baker," Colt replied, nodding toward her.

Griff Waters studied them both for a moment before he spoke. When he did finally speak, his words came out slowly. "Oh, yeah, I remember you. You're the cop that sent my boy home in a box. In that case, you can call me Mr. Waters." He paused. "Or better yet, don't call me at all, cop."

Lauren could see Colt's back tense visibly. She longed to reach out and touch him, to offer him some kind of support, even if it was only through a simple touch. But she couldn't move. She could hardly breathe.

"We need to talk to you about Dillon," Colt said, his voice sounding tight and controlled. He didn't bother to tell Griff he was no longer a cop, and Lauren didn't see any reason to tell him, either.

"There ain't nothing to say. My boy's already dead. Now get out of here," he ordered.

Colt turned his head slightly, as though he could no longer hold the man's gaze and had to think hard about his next words. "No," he said finally. "We need to talk first."

"I don't talk to cops. Now get off my property."

He started to slam the door.

"We have reason to believe Dillon isn't dead."

Griff Waters stopped and pulled the door open again. "What did you say, cop?"

"Mr. Waters, your son may be alive."

"If this is some sort of a joke, I'm not laughing."

"It's not a joke, Mr. Waters. There's been a man fitting your son's description threatening the safety of some of the residents around Rock Hill. And I want to know if you've seen anyone who reminds you of Dillon, or if anyone has come here to see you."

"Ain't nobody been here but you," the older man snapped. "And the last time I saw my boy was when I opened that box you sent him in so that I could make sure it was my boy I was putting in the ground and not some bum from out there in California."

"You're sure?"

"Of course I'm sure. Just as I'm sure you cops tried to pin something on my boy. Something to make him look bad so as to cover up the mistake you made in shooting him. You cops are all the same. Always covering things up. Always doing one thing, then writing down something else in all those reports you fill out. Always sticking together to make innocent people look bad, thinking it will make you all look better.

"Well, it won't," he rambled on. "I know how you all do things. And it don't matter what you say or what you write in some stupid report. My boy was a good boy. I taught him to be a good boy. And you cops had to go and shoot him. For no reason."

Lauren suddenly stopped listening, realizing that she'd been so caught up in the man's rambling that she'd forgotten to pay attention to everything else around her. Dillon Waters could have come walking up right behind her and she would never have known it until she felt his knife in her back. She looked behind her to make sure he wasn't there. And though she didn't see him, she had the strange feeling that he was coming closer. Was it her imagination or had the curtain hanging in one of the windows of the trailer just moved? Someone was in there, watching them. She was almost certain of it.

"Colt..." she said softly. She finally gave in to her need to touch him and reached up, placing her hand on his back. Her hands were cold and clammy, and the warmth of him touched her through the softness of his shirt. "Let's go. He can't help us."

"Yeah," Colt muttered.

"Is your woman sick?" Griff Waters asked. "She looks like death warmed over."

Colt stepped down off the trailer's bottom step and turned toward the cycle, pulling Lauren with him. Neither of them offered him any reply.

Death warmed over. What a choice of words, Lauren thought, allowing another shudder to pass through her. She did feel a little weak and cold inside. But then, she hadn't slept well, and that small ache in her head still lingered, despite the aspirin she'd taken. Was she coming down with the flu or could Dillon Waters have something to do with the state of her health? Her heart picked up its pace just from thinking about it.

"You wait just a minute, cop!" Griff's voice had risen sharply, and it stopped them both. "You think you can just come and go as you please, do you? Well, you're wrong. You came here, and now you're going to listen to what I have to say."

Colt stopped and turned back to the old man. "Unless you're going to tell me you've seen someone who looks like your son, and you know where he is, we've got nothing more to discuss," Colt replied evenly.

"Oh, yes, cop, I know where my son is," said Griff. He grinned, revealing two missing teeth.

"Where?" Colt asked evenly.

Lauren couldn't see Colt's face, but the controlled tightness in that single word told her that Colt knew Griff Waters was playing games with them.

"At the Holly Hill Cemetery," Griff told them. "Plot number 217."

Lauren closed her eyes briefly and let out a sigh. She didn't appreciate this game between the two men. She needed out of here. She needed to sit down and rest.

Then she heard the laughter.

Her eyes snapped open and she looked around. The laughter stopped. Except for the stillness, the absence of birdsong, there was no sign of anything out of the ordinary. "Did you hear that?" Lauren asked Colt softly.

"Hear what?" he replied softly.

"Nothing," she muttered, not wanting to explain in front of Griff Waters. And yet she still felt it. She felt that someone was watching. She felt eyes watching her from all directions. Dillon Waters was close, and coming closer with each passing second. He was watching her. She could feel him closing in, almost as surely as she could remember his cold touch from the night before.

Colt gave her hand a squeeze and turned toward the motorcycle.

"Maybe while you're out there paying your respects to my boy, you can do your job as a cop and find out who vandalized that place." Griff Waters's words stopped them both a second time, and together they turned to face him.

"Someone vandalized the cemetery?" Colt asked quietly.

"Sure did," replied Griff. "Looks like there must have been a bunch of them in on it, too, because if there was only one, he had to be pretty strong and really crazy. And he must have used something big, like a sledgehammer or something."

Lauren remembered what Dillon Waters's grip had felt like when he tried to strangle her. There was no doubt in her mind that he was pretty strong. And there was no question at all that he was really crazy.

"When did this happen?" Colt asked the older man.

"Hell if I know. I went to the cemetery yesterday afternoon to put flowers on my boy's grave, and the place was a mess."

"Did you report this to anyone?" Colt was still holding her hand, his words precise and even. He still seemed relaxed, but Lauren could feel the tension in his hand, and she knew that he was doing his best to hide it from Griff Waters.

Lauren gripped his hand in return, her anxiety and the need to leave growing stronger and stronger.

"There wasn't anyone around," Griff replied. "I don't know where the caretaker was. It was the first time I've ever been there to visit my boy's grave that I haven't seen him around."

"Thanks," said Colt.

"Oh, yeah, sure," said Griff sarcastically. "You're welcome, all right. And thank you for taking my boy from me. Anytime you want to come by again, you just feel free. We'll crack open a few beers and have a real talk! Maybe we could watch a ball game or two together! What do you say?"

Lauren and Colt turned away, leaving the old man to continue his rambling. Lauren's headache was growing. And the coldness inside her seemed to have settled in the pit of her stomach.

She leaned forward and rested her face against Colt's back as they rode away from Griff Waters's trailer. That place was bound to show up in her nightmares, and she hoped she'd never have to venture down this way again.

"Where are we going?" she asked over the roar of the motorcycle. She had the feeling she knew—she just hoped she was wrong.

"To the Holly Hill Cemetery," he replied.

She hadn't been wrong. She sighed and tried to swallow down the lump that had risen in her throat. The last thing she needed right now was a cemetery. It was just another thing to remind her of how close her own death might be.

It wasn't long before they reached the large iron gates of the cemetery. They were open, and Colt steered the motorcycle slowly through them.

They stopped just inside the cemetery and climbed off the bike.

"Look at this place," Lauren whispered, pulling off the helmet. "It's a mess."

She hadn't needed to say it. Colt was already looking around.

Set back off the main highway in a large grove of trees, the Holly Hill Cemetery couldn't be seen from the highway, so the damage would have gone unreported until someone actually came to visit a grave. And because it was a fairly small cemetery, set outside of town, it could be a few days before anyone came by.

Colt leaned down to examine a headstone. "The old man was right. It looks as though someone took a sledgehammer to this one."

At least the breeze was blowing here, and the birds were singing in the trees. Still, Lauren felt a chill pass through her. She crossed her arms against it and moved closer to Colt. "Dillon Waters did this," she said softly.

Colt didn't reply right away. "I wouldn't be surprised if old Griff did this himself," he muttered, refusing to believe Dillon Waters could do this in death. His eyes met hers briefly before he moved on to examine another headstone. "Not all of them are destroyed," he pointed out.

Lauren's gaze swept along the rows of headstones. "No, they're not, are they? It looks almost like a line has been destroyed—or a path."

"Let's see where it leads," Colt said.

Lauren didn't want to follow Colt. She knew Dillon had something to do with the vandalism, and she had no desire to see what he'd left for her at the end of this grotesque path.

But she had no choice. Colt held the rifle in one hand and took hers in his other. They moved slowly past the chipped and broken headstones, always looking to make sure nothing—no one—hid behind them.

"This gives me the creeps," Lauren said softly.

"I agree. There's too many trees, too many large headstones. Too many places for someone to hide."

They passed a headstone on which so much of the name had been broken away that they couldn't even read it.

"It seems to be getting worse," Colt told her.

So was the cold, sick terror within her, but Lauren didn't tell him that.

They reached the end of the path of vandalism, and Colt stopped so suddenly that Lauren bumped into him. When she got her bearings once again, she followed his gaze, looking down at the headstone before her.

This one wasn't chipped or hammered in any way. It was Dillon Waters's headstone. The inscription carved into it was pure and simple and straightforward, giving his name, Dillon Robert Waters—the year of his birth, and the date of his death—October 17, just slightly more than six months before. Something about the date of his death touched Lauren, but she didn't dwell on it. She wasn't given the chance. Her gaze moved lower. And what she saw caused her knees to go so weak they threatened to give out beneath her. She gripped Colt's hand, knowing that any moment she was going to fall.

Looking at his headstone, seeing his name cut into the stone, would have been enough to make her shiver. But it was what had been added to the headstone that caused her to shudder.

Dillon Waters's headstone had been sprayed with red paint. Beside his name, something had been drawn in the same bloodred paint.

It was a heart.

And in the middle of it was *her* name.

CHAPTER NINE

For the first time in her life, Lauren thought she might faint.

"Lauren?" She could feel Colt squeeze her hand tightly. His voice sounded so far away. "Red?"

She sucked in a deep breath, and the darkness that had overtaken her began to fade away. Though she hadn't truly fainted, her brain still refused to function correctly. The sunlight that filtered through the trees hurt her eyes. Tiny starlike speckles danced above Colt's head when she looked up at him. Still, she never took her eyes off of his face. It was so much easier to look at him than to look at her name on that tombstone. She concentrated on his hand holding hers. It felt so strong, so warm, so stable when the whole rest of the world seemed to be collapsing.

"Oh, Colt..." she moaned softly.

"Try to relax," Colt replied. "And take a deep breath."

The deep breath was easy, but Lauren had the feeling she'd never be able to relax again. The coldness had swept through her, taking over, leaving nothing. She felt hollow, empty. It was almost as though death had already claimed her, sweeping her life from her. She leaned against Colt, reaching for his warmth, reaching for life, for something that could wipe away the terror that filled her.

She knew Dillon Waters wanted to kill her. But until this moment, she hadn't realized the intensity of his need to have her dead.

She couldn't help but look down at her name once again. The red paint had dripped, and it looked more like blood than paint. Droplets of the paint cascaded from every letter of her name. And the heart looked more as if it, too, were bleeding.

Lauren took another deep breath. "Where do you suppose he is right now?" she asked in a quiet voice.

Colt glanced around. "I wish I knew."

Lauren looked around, as well, knowing what Colt was thinking. They were out in the open, and Dillon Waters could be hiding behind any tree or any large headstone. Just because the birds were singing and Lauren didn't feel Dillon's presence, that didn't mean he wasn't close.

"What are we going to do?" Lauren's voice was hardly more than a whisper. She leaned her head on his shoulder. Hearing his heartbeat, she tried to concentrate on it, just as she had the other times when she'd heard it and it had brought stable comfort. Why couldn't it seem to bring her any now?

"There's an office over there." Colt used the rifle to point through the trees. "There should be a phone. We need to call the police and report this damage."

"Are we going to tell them that Dillon Waters is trying to kill me? I doubt they'll believe us after they read his name on the tombstone," Lauren said. Her voice never rose. The terror vibrating through her was just too strong. She didn't have the strength for anything else.

"No, but we will tell them someone has been harassing you."

Lauren laughed bitterly at his words. "Harassing me," she echoed, her voice still flat. "Is that what he's doing to me? I've got a dead dog, a gash on my hand. Not to mention the little things, like broken dishes and skinned knees. And even Griff Waters wondered whether I was sick. I look like I haven't slept in a week—or like I'm already dead."

"Lauren . . ." he cut in.

She went on as though he hadn't spoken. "Or haven't you looked at me lately? Maybe I am already dead and I just don't know it yet."

"Lauren..." he said again. There was laughter in his voice. "That's the damnedest thing I've ever heard."

"And what about the dark circles around my eyes? I look like a raccoon."

"Lauren!"

"It's not such a crazy idea. I mean, Dillon Waters is running around as though he doesn't realize he's supposed to be dead. Why shouldn't I be the same way?"

He laughed wholeheartedly then.

"I don't think it's funny, Colt."

His laughter died away, and he grew serious. "What happened to that woman yesterday who lectured me on life, who told me she could never give up?" His hand left her back, and he reached up to gently cup her cheek and hold her face close to his. "What happened to her?"

Lauren swallowed hard. "She got scared," she whispered.

"With good reason," he replied. "But that's not enough to make her give up, is it?" He was so close, close enough to make her forget the dangers that lurked just outside the circle of the two of them.

"No," she whispered.

"I didn't think so," he said softly. "We're going to get through this, Red."

She could only nod at his words. The pressure of his hand on her cheek increased slightly, and he drew closer, mere inches closer, to reach her lips, to take possession of her mouth.

His mouth was so warm, so utterly right, so perfect. There was no hunger in the kiss, but there was compassion, softness and a tenderness that caused her knees to go weak.

He pulled away reluctantly. "I know you said you were scared, but try to remember that Waters is just *trying* to scare you. It's what he wants."

She nodded again. "Well, he's doing a hell of a job. But he also wants me dead." She threw a glance toward Dillon Waters's headstone.

It was Colt's turn to glance at the headstone, taking in her name. "Why do you think he wants you dead, Lauren?"

"Because he's dead, and he loves me. He wants me with him," she replied flatly.

Colt had a hard time accepting the idea, so he didn't reply. He suddenly didn't even care about the *why* of it all. He only cared about the woman in his arms. He intended to do whatever it took to keep Waters from getting to her. At first, he'd chosen to help Lauren just to keep her away from Waters. It really had nothing to do with Lauren herself.

Now, Colt realized, keeping Waters from getting his hands on Lauren had everything to do with her. Never mind what had happened between Colt and Dillon in the past. This was the present, and it had everything to do with Colt keeping Lauren. He couldn't lose her. Not now.

"Come on," he said. "I don't like standing out in the open like this. Let's get out of here." Colt took her hand again as they moved toward the office.

They reached the door to the office and found it standing open by a few inches. Colt lightly touched the door with the tip of the rifle and started to push it open.

"Wait!" she said urgently, stopping him. Her whisper echoed loudly, and she realized with a sense of foreboding that the birds were no longer singing. The area around them had grown completely quiet.

"What?" Colt asked. The end of the rifle was against the door. One slight push and the door would be open.

And then Lauren knew. Dillon Waters was in there, waiting for her.

The door opened on its own. With a loud, continuous creak, it widened slowly, allowing the sunlight to drift into the small, dark room.

Lauren let out a cry. Inside the room, sitting behind a small desk, was a man, apparently the caretaker of the cemetery. His dead eyes saw nothing, and yet they still seemed to be looking at Lauren.

The handle of a knife, the same knife Dillon Waters had tried to kill Lauren with, the knife she recognized from her own kitchen, protruded from his throat. Blood, looking no different from the paint on the tombstone, dripped down his neck into the collar of his shirt.

Colt let go of Lauren's hand and pulled her tightly against him, pressing her face into his shoulder so that she didn't have to look. Hell, he wished more than he had ever wished for anything that he could shelter her from this. He wished he could just hold her in his arms forever and keep her from everything but himself. Her moan was muffled against his shirt, and she drew in great gulps of air.

"He's—" she began.

"Yeah. He's dead," Colt said quietly.

He stepped into the room, taking her with him.

"No!" She brought her arms around him tightly. "Don't go in there!" She turned her head enough to take in the small room. There was nothing to look at but the dead man behind the desk.

"We have to," Colt told her. "We have to call the police, and the only phone is in here."

"No," she argued. "Dillon could still be inside."

He moved her out of his arms just a bit so that he stood inside the threshold, while she still remained outside.

"There's no one here, Lauren. We can see the whole room."

"I don't want to be in there with him," she said.

"Don't look at him."

"That's easy for you to say. You might be used to seeing dead people, but I'm not. And there's nowhere else to look in there," she replied, her voice rising again. Tears came to her eyes. "I've never seen anything so horrible, Colt."

"Would you rather wait outside for me?" he asked, when she was silent for a moment.

"No!"

"Why don't you stand right here in the doorway, then? He's not in here, so you can stand and look outside."

"All right," she finally agreed. She was still reluctant to let Colt go, however. She grasped his hand when he moved away to reach for the phone, and she held it until he slipped from her grasp.

She wanted to turn and look at him, but she forced herself to keep her eyes outside. Behind her, she could hear him lift the receiver and begin to speak quietly, though she didn't listen to his actual words.

Outside, the sun was shining brightly, filtering through the trees that blew in the soft breeze. It was a beautiful day. Almost beautiful enough to help her forget all her fears.

She leaned against the doorjamb and took a deep breath, wishing she could just go home and forget everything that had happened. She wished she could get back to planting her flower bulbs. She wished she could start over with Colt, that the two of them could have a chance to see where their feelings led.

Lauren?

She stiffened and a tingle moved up her spine at the sound of her whispered name. "Colt..." she whispered.

No, don't think of him, Dillon whispered.

She ignored the command. "Colt, Colt..." She wasn't even sure whether she spoke out loud or not. Her heart was pounding in her chest, sounding so loud in her ears that she couldn't seem to hear her own voice. She looked down, noticing the uneven, worn boards of the porch.

Look at me, Dillon said.

She could hear his whispers so clearly. He was so close. She could feel his cold presence right in front of her.

Lauren, look at me, he said again.

She stared at her feet. "No," she whispered. "Leave me alone."

I can't. I love you too much. I want you too much.

She thought she could feel his breath on her face, but she refused to look up. "I don't want you," she whispered firmly. She couldn't seem to get her words to come out any louder. "Colt."

Dillon's hand came into her line of vision, and he touched her fingers. Instinctively she pulled her hand away.

Look at me now. Come away with me now, and I'll forgive you for being with Norbrook. And I won't kill him.

She shook her head. "No." Her strength was ebbing away. Terror was gripping her, clenching around her middle like the strong jaws of a shark. It was biting into her, making it harder and harder for her to breathe, making it harder and harder for her to continue looking down.

Look at me, love, he said tenderly.

She almost did. Almost. It was so hard not to.

Then she closed her eyes, briefly, just to keep from looking up. "Leave me alone," she said slowly. Her voice sounded harsh and breathy. "Colt," she said again, or thought she did. Perhaps she was only thinking the words, for he didn't seem to be hearing her. She tried to turn and look at him, but she was frozen with fear, and her feet refused to move.

Dillon chuckled softly. *He's a liar, Lauren. He'll hurt you in the end.*

"No," she said, refusing to believe it. She tried to dwell on thoughts of Colt's last kiss. It had been so filled with tenderness.

Yes, he will, and deep down you know it, too, don't you?

"Go away," she said. Her strength was nearly gone, and she could hardly hear her own words.

You're not as strong as you think you are, my love. Look at me. You are mine. You can't win.

Lauren had no idea where the courage came from, but she welcomed it. She remembered Colt's words reminding her of the woman of yesterday, the woman who had refused to give up. "No," she said, with as much force as she could muster. "I am stronger than you. I'll be as strong as I have to in order to beat you. I'm not going to let you win. I'm not going to let you kill me. I'll never be yours. I belong with Colt."

He laughed sarcastically, and the sound of it echoed through her, mixed with horror. *I told you, you can't trust him. He'll just hurt you.*

"No, he won't," she argued.

Ask him about me, love. He hasn't told you the whole truth. He hasn't told you everything. His cold fingertips gently caressed her cheek, and she turned away from him. The side of her face bumped into the wall of the office. *Go ahead. Ask him.*

Her head still turned to the side, Lauren braved a glance ahead of her, noticing that the trees were once again blowing in the breeze. The soft sounds of the birds chirping touched her ears, and she was suddenly aware of the way she was panting, trying to catch her breath.

A hand touched her shoulder. "Lauren?"

She started and let out a cry of alarm.

"Lauren, it's just me," Colt said. "What's the matter?"

"He was here," she said softly. Her strength finally left her, and she leaned against him. His arm came around her protectively. "He was right here in front of me. He talked to me. He touched my cheek," she explained.

"Lauren, there's no one here."

"Surely you must have seen him. He was here just a second ago. He couldn't have gotten away that quickly without you seeing him," she persisted.

"I didn't see anyone, and I still don't."

His chin touched the top of her head, and she felt him turn as he looked around.

"I'm telling you, he was here."

"Lauren." He shifted, grasped her upper arms and turned her around to face him. "He couldn't have been here, I would have seen him or heard him. I didn't."

She shook her head slowly, not wanting to believe him. Dillon had told her Colt was a liar. And he had to be lying to her now. He had to be. If he was telling the truth, then she had lost her sanity.

She saw something else in Colt's eyes. He firmly believed what he was saying. He hadn't seen or heard Dillon Waters. She knew it was useless to try to convince him otherwise. Oh, God, she really must be losing her mind. She pressed her face against Colt's shoulder and clung to him as tightly as she could. "Hold me. Just hold me."

He held her quietly, his embrace warm and strong.

"What took you so long on the phone?" she asked quietly.

"What? I wasn't talking for more than a minute."

"It seemed so much longer," she muttered.

"Well, it wasn't," he replied. He let her go just enough that he could step out the door and close it. Lauren watched him until her gaze took in the dead caretaker behind the desk and she forced herself to look away.

It was almost comical, she thought, how Dillon Waters had filled her with so much fear that she'd been able to forget about the caretaker.

"Are we going to wait for the police?" she asked.

"No." He took her hand and started to lead her back toward his motorcycle.

Lauren didn't feel as anxious as they retraced their steps. The birds were singing, the wind was blowing. She didn't feel Dillon's presence any longer.

"I didn't tell them my name," said Colt. "And I just reported that I'd come here to visit the grave of a dead relative when I noticed some of the tombstones had been vandalized. I figured I'd let them find the caretaker on their own. I didn't think either one of us was up to answering a lot a questions right now."

"They may question me anyway. It's my knife sticking out of him," she told Colt.

"You're sure?" He never paused as they maneuvered their way around the headstones heading toward the entrance to the cemetery, but he turned and looked at her.

"Yes. It has my initials carved into the handle. It's the same one Dillon used to stab Mav and try to kill me with yesterday," she explained.

Colt stopped walking and turned around, moving quickly in the opposite direction.

"What are you doing?" she asked, not letting go of his hand, moving right with him.

"Going back for the knife," he said shortly.

"But you can't just take it," she argued. "It's evidence. If you take it and they find out, then we'd really be suspects."

He stopped so suddenly that she bumped right into him. "If they find out it's your knife, you will definitely be a suspect. They'll take you in for questioning. They may even arrest you. And I'm not a cop anymore, so I won't be able to help you. I probably won't even be able to stay with you. Don't you see? You'll be a sitting target, just waiting for Waters to come and nab you."

"But this is wrong," she told him.

"This is just another way of protecting you."

"But I didn't kill him."

"Do you think the police are going to simply believe you? Like they believed you when you told them someone was trying to kill you?" he asked, his eyes never leaving hers.

"But it's wrong for us to take it. It makes me look guilty," she told him. "And I'm not."

They resumed their half walk, half run to the office.

"I know that, and you know that. All we're doing is fixing it so that the police won't connect you with any of this. Now come on, they'll be here any minute."

"You don't think they're going to connect me to any of this?" she questioned, letting out a sarcastic chuckle. "When my name's painted on a tombstone?"

"Just make sure you act surprised if they come to the inn and ask you about it," Colt put in.

"Sounds easy," she muttered.

"Piece of cake," he replied. "Come on."

When they reached the office, Colt used a white handkerchief he'd pulled from his back pocket to open the door and then wipe the knob clean. He left Lauren standing in the doorway and entered the office where he also wiped his fingerprints from the phone. Then he used the handkerchief to grasp the handle of the knife.

As he pulled the knife free, the caretaker's head fell back to rest in an odd position against the back of the chair. Quickly, Colt retraced his steps back to where Lauren was standing. He would have taken her hand again, but his were full—the knife in one and his rifle in the other. Lauren simply followed him out the door, leaving it open behind them.

They ran past the rows of headstones to the entrance of the cemetery. When they had reached his motorcycle, he slipped the rifle into its pouch and handed the bloodied knife to Lauren. "Hold this."

Whether it was wrapped in a handkerchief or not, she didn't want to touch it, and she groaned down at it.

"I'm sorry, Lauren," he said, "but I can't drive and hold on to it at the same time."

Reluctantly she held it as she climbed onto the bike behind him. She wrapped it completely in the handkerchief, cringing as the blood from the blade seeped through the cotton, and held it as far away from her body as possible.

In the distance, they could hear the siren of an approaching police car. Colt tried to start the motorcycle.

And nothing happened.

CHAPTER TEN

"**W**hat's the matter with it?" Lauren yelled.

"I don't know."

The sound of the siren was growing closer with each passing moment.

He tried to start the bike again, and still nothing happened.

A wave of anxious fear washed over Lauren, and her eyes were drawn to the curve of the road, where she knew she would soon be seeing the police car. What then? she wondered. She and Colt would be questioned. They'd be forced to explain the guns and the knife. Then, when the caretaker's body was found, they'd surely be arrested. She closed her eyes for a moment against that thought.

"Do you think Dillon Waters did something to it?"

"Dillon Waters isn't here," he replied.

But he was, she thought. He was....

The cycle sputtered and came to life on the third try. And Colt whisked them off in the opposite direction from the approaching police car, so suddenly that Lauren had to grab him around the waist to keep from flying off, the knife nearly slipping from her hand.

"Do you think they saw us?" she asked, once they were some distance away.

He shook his head. "I doubt it," he said, talking loudly over the sound of the engine so that she could hear him without his having to turn toward her. "I think we were far enough away that the trees hid us."

She let out a long sign of hopeful relief and gently leaned her cheek against his back. She wished the two of them could keep riding as they were—riding into the sunset, never looking back. Riding off to a place where they never had to worry about Dillon Waters or the police or the dead caretaker or anything.

But, alas, this was reality. Riding off into the sunset on a horse—or a motorcycle, as the case might be—only happened in the movies. And she had the terrible feeling that no matter where they went, Dillon Waters would find them. He always seemed to know where she was.

Colt drove the motorcycle into nearby Rock Hill Recreational Park. "Are you all right?" he asked, killing the engine and finally turning to speak.

She continued to hold one arm around his waist, while she gripped the knife in her other hand. "Yes," she replied honestly. Oddly enough, she did feel fine. Here in the park, she didn't feel Dillon Waters's presence, and she felt secure. "What are we going to do with this?" she asked, holding up the knife where he could see it. "Throw it in the lake?"

"No," he replied, glancing at the knife before turning slightly to look back at her. "I haven't been here that long, and already I've seen the lake get dragged twice. If the police ever found this, they might just be bored enough to check it out."

"Well, what am I going to do with it, then?" she asked, finally climbing off the motorcycle to stand and stare at him. They were almost at eye level. The sun was in her eyes when she looked at him. His eyes were shadowed, but still they sparkled with the warmth she recognized as his alone. She would probably have moved closer to him right then, if not for the looming presence of the bloody knife she held. Just the feel of it in her hand was enough to make her knees go weak.

"We're going to take it home and run it through your dishwasher, and you're going to put it back with the rest of the knives."

She laughed sarcastically. "You're kidding, right? You don't really expect me to use this ever again, do you?"

"I don't care if you use it again or not. But I don't want it found anywhere where it can be connected to the caretaker's murder," he said. His eyes still sparkled, and Lauren found it hard to look away. "Now stop holding it up where anyone can see it, and give it to me so I can put it someplace."

She gladly handed it to him. Though there was no blood on the handle and the handkerchief had protected her, her hand still felt dirty. She rubbed her hands together in an attempt to erase the lingering, nasty feeling.

His eyes left hers for the first time as he leaned away to slide the knife into the pouch with the rifle.

"Isn't this called tampering with evidence or obstructing justice or something?" she asked.

"It's called saving your life," he replied.

He turned back to her, and the expression on his face reminded her of the way he'd looked before he made love to her. He reached out and took her uninjured hand. His touch sent a wave of heat and tenderness through her. "You and I both know you didn't kill that man. But because it's your knife—and I'm willing to bet my bottom dollar that the only fingerprints on it are yours—it'd be a little hard to prove in a court just how it got from your kitchen to the cemetery. Especially with your name painted on a tombstone."

"What are we going to do?" she asked quietly.

"What do you want to do?" His voice was soft, filled with a compassion in which she knew she could easily get lost.

"I want to go home," she said simply. She had to stop herself from adding "and make love with you again." She would have liked nothing better than to curl up in his arms and have him hold her and touch her and love her. But she was still uncertain of his feelings for her, and feared confessing such a desire. "I want to go back to my place and clean it up. And take a shower. And eat a hot bowl of chicken noodle soup before I snuggle up on the couch and sleep."

His eyes never left hers. Nor did their tenderness and warmth. She wondered how he'd react had she told him what she really wanted.

"What about Dillon Waters?" he asked.

Lauren didn't understand where her courage was coming from, but it *was* coming, and it was growing stronger, and she welcomed it like a warm touch of sunshine on a cool day. "I want him," she said. "I want him to come for me so I can fight him and stop him for good. And I think it's best to have the home-field advantage, don't you?"

Colt's hand tightened on hers. "I don't know," he said softly. "I don't know how we can even begin to fight him. I don't like the thought of him getting anywhere near you."

"Neither do I," she admitted. "But I'm tired of constantly looking over my shoulder. I'm tired of being afraid, of hearing his voice and feeling his presence." She held Colt's gaze. "I want him out of my life.

For good.'' And I want you in it, she thought. But I'll never know if I can really have you until Waters is gone for good.

"Do you plan to kill him?" Colt asked simply.

She shrugged slightly. "I don't plan to do anything. I mean, I don't even know what to plan. I shot him five times yesterday and he got right back up. So how could I kill him? What do I plan next? Should I drop a concrete block on his head from ten stories up? Maybe he's some kind of robot, and all I have to do is find the right switch to turn. Or maybe he really is some sort of ghost, and I need a ghost hunter."

Colt seemed to recognize her need to talk, and he didn't interrupt. He just gazed at her intently, listening to her words and looking at her as though he really liked what he was seeing. The fact was, he did like what he was seeing. He liked it a lot. Despite her pallor and the dark circles under her eyes, she was everything he'd ever wanted in a woman.

"If he is a ghost," she went on, "if Dillon Waters is really dead, then any earthly thing we do, like shooting him or stabbing him, isn't going to work, right?" She couldn't believe she was talking like this. She couldn't believe she was rationally discussing killing a man who might possibly already be dead. "It's all just a little bit crazy, isn't it?"

He knew full well what she meant. He recognized the look in her eyes. He recognized her need to speak and be heard. Six months ago, he'd seen it in his own eyes. Only there had been no one to listen to him, and he'd been forced to give up everything he thought was important because he couldn't let any of his built-up feelings out. Her words brought him back to the present.

"The fact is, everything we know tells us Dillon Waters is dead. And yet here he is. Right here among us. It was hard enough dealing with the fact that someone wanted to kill me. That someone would go so far as to tamper with the brakes on my truck and the gas line to the inn just to hurt me. No, not hurt me—kill me," she corrected. "Do you know how hard it is trying to convince myself that the man who wants me dead is dead himself? That the police can't help me? That there's no place I can go that would make me feel safe?"

"I've got a pretty good idea," he muttered.

She continued as though he hadn't spoken. "And then there's you."

"What about me?" he asked, a spark of interest flickering in his eyes.

"You haven't been honest with me. You say all sorts of things that don't make any sense. You leave me with a lot of unanswered questions. I hardly know you, and still I trusted you enough to go to bed with you. And you haven't said a word about it. God, how could I have been so stupid?" She had no answer to that question, and yet she knew without a doubt that she wanted him still. She knew that all he would have to do was take her in his arms again, and she'd be his, no matter how often her brain told her it was stupid. She simply had no control over her responses to him.

She was rambling on as though a dam had broken and there was no longer any stopping the flood. "What was I thinking? I never even thought to say no. I never even thought about contraception. I never thought how we would feel the next morning."

"How haven't I been honest with you?" he asked quietly. Her first statement had grabbed him so completely that he had hardly heard the rest of her rambling.

"I don't know," she said, stopping suddenly, his question taking hold of her.

"Then why would you think I haven't been honest?"

"Dillon told me," she answered without thinking.

His brows rose in question and surprise. "He did? When?"

Lauren had to think for a moment. "I—" she began, not sure just how to reply. She couldn't remember whether it had been a dream or she had just imagined it. The answer came to her so suddenly, she wondered why she hadn't been able to remember before. "When you were in the caretaker's office. He told me to ask you about him. He said you hadn't told me everything about him. Which, by the way, doesn't surprise me at all."

His eyes left hers suddenly, as though he didn't have the strength or the courage to look her in the eye. And that was just enough to tell her that her words were true, that Dillon Waters had told her the truth. There was more that Colt was keeping from her. And still he said nothing.

"Tell me," she said. For a long moment, there was silence between them, and Lauren thought again of his words. *Destiny be damned*. Just what did that mean? Why did this man before her have to be such a mystery? Why couldn't he be as open to her with his thoughts and his past as he was when he made love to her? She needed some answers before she went absolutely crazy. "Please tell me," she nearly begged him. "I feel like I'm wandering around in the dark looking for a way out that I'll never be able to find. For crying out loud, Dillon Waters wants to kill us both. If there's a reason other than his love for me—''

"Do you really think that's why he wants to kill you?'' Colt said, interrupting her.

"It's what he keeps telling me,'' she replied. "Not that I think it's enough reason to take another person's life. But if there's more, then I deserve to know.''

Colt had no reply.

Lauren looked into his eyes, and saw his struggle. He wanted to tell her—and yet he couldn't.

"Fine,'' she said finally. "Don't tell me. Keep me in the dark. I love mysteries. And you, Colt, are the biggest mystery in my life.'' She let go of his hand and turned away, heading farther into the park, toward the pavilions and the playground.

"Where are you going?'' he yelled at her, jumping off the motorcycle to go after her.

"Over there to watch the ball game,'' she yelled back, without turning to look at him. She wanted to get away from him, away from the confusion he brought her. She should be safe in the crowd.

"What about Waters?'' he called out, trying to catch up to her.

"At least he's been honest with me. He told me he wants to kill me, and I firmly believe he does.''

Colt finally reached her side, but she didn't hesitate in her stride. He reached out and grasped her elbow, forcing her to stop and look at him.

"No, I mean what will you do when he comes back and tries to kill you again?'' he asked, his eyes piercing hers.

She swallowed hard, then lifted her chin. "Just what do you care?''

"I do care.''

"Oh, yeah? Right. Well, I don't need your mysterious caring attitude," she snapped. She also didn't need the way he looked at her, the way he made her feel as if her insides were melting. She didn't need his kisses. And she especially didn't need the memories she couldn't put aside of their night of lovemaking. But she knew she was only lying to herself—she did need the kisses and the memories. And yet, she didn't tell him any of that. "I can take care of myself."

He was going to laugh at that. Lauren could see the amusement in his eyes. She waited for the laughter to reach her. She waited, struggling with the mad urge to slap his face.

But the laughter never came, though the amusement never completely left his eyes. "And I suppose lying on the floor bleeding, with a man holding a knife over you, is your way of taking care of yourself?" he asked her.

She pulled out of his grasp. "Why don't you just stop reminding me of my incompetence?"

"I'm not trying to remind you of your incompetence. I'm only trying to remind you of who and what it is we're dealing with here." His voice softened. "We're going to deal with this together, Lauren. I'm not leaving you, no matter what."

"Why not?" she asked softly, wanting to hear him say that he loved her, or at least that he wanted her.

"Because you're wearing my shirt." He gently touched the soft cotton covering her arm.

She turned to face him squarely, and in a sudden rush of anger began to undo the buttons. "Well, here, have it back, then." She had every intention of stripping it off and throwing the damned garment in his face.

His hands moved to stop hers. "I don't want it back, Lauren. I want you to have it."

She looked up into his eyes. "But you said . . ."

"I know what I said, but I didn't mean I wanted it back. I want you to keep it. I want to see you wear it after every time I make love with you."

She could only stare at him. His words left her feeling slightly dizzy. He was giving her a promise of more nights like last night. He was giving her a promise of tomorrow.

"I know I never said a word about last night," he went on. "Because I felt words weren't necessary. I didn't think there were words to describe what you gave me last night."

Lauren blinked at him, wondering if she'd heard right, wondering just what it was that she'd given him last night. "What exactly did I give you?"

"Something I haven't felt in a very long time. My soul."

His words made even less sense than before. "What?"

"Tell me you understand that I can't leave you," he said gently. Reaching out slowly, he caressed her jaw. He slid his hand smoothly down her throat, and his fingers pressed gently against her beating pulse.

"Yes," she whispered. "I understand." His reasons were the same as hers. He, too, had given her back her soul.

He gently drew her into his embrace and held her to his chest, where she heard his heart beating in unison with hers. For several long moments, neither of them moved. The breeze blew around them, picking up strength with the approach of another evening storm.

"We'd better go," he said, his words breaking through the spell of safety and compassion his arms had woven around her.

"Where?" she asked quietly, not moving out of his embrace.

She heard the intake of air in his lungs as he took a deep breath. "Back to your inn," he replied. "That is where you said you wanted to go, isn't it?"

"Yes."

"Then we'll go together. We'll wait for Dillon Waters together."

She met his gaze, wondering if he had any idea what his words meant to her.

He held her hand as they walked back to the motorcycle. The strength of his grip told her he wasn't about to let her go.

He climbed on and handed her the helmet.

"When we get back," she said, looking at him, not yet putting on the helmet, "will you tell me the truth about your connection to Dillon Waters?"

"What exactly do you want to know?"

She contemplated each word before she spoke. "Did you arrest him or something when you were a cop in Los Angeles? Or was the bank robbery the first time you ever saw him?"

He looked back at her and met her eyes. The intense look he gave her seemed hot enough to burn her soul. She couldn't have looked away if her life had depended on it.

"Yes, I arrested him once. Not that it did any good," he said quietly. "And later, I shot him."

"You? I know you said it was your team that—"

"It was my task force that was assigned to bring him out, but I was the sniper with my sights set on him. And it was my bullet that took him down." It was the first real blaze of heated emotion, the first unmasked emotion, aside from passion, that she'd seen from him, and it was somewhat frightening. But his next words scared her even more. "I fired all six shots into him. And the only thing I'm sorry about is the fact that I didn't know to save one for myself."

a warmth that frightening. Still she went ahead, and lost herself in the rich taste of him. Finally she drew away. "I'm sorry about what happened that I don't know you, and I..."

CHAPTER ELEVEN

"Colt..." She said only his name, not knowing what else to say.

"Get on the motorcycle," he said shortly. "If we're going back to your inn, I want to get there before it rains. I want to check everything out and make sure Waters isn't hiding somewhere."

Slowly Lauren put the helmet over her head, contemplating Colt's words. There were hundreds of places Dillon Waters could hide around the inn. The stable, the wooded paths winding around the lake, the boat dock, the pool. Not to mention the inn itself. Lauren thought of the musty, dark basement that she always tried to avoid, and for a moment thought of telling Colt she'd changed her mind about returning.

Then she found her courage. She wasn't going to let Dillon Waters scare her out of her own home. She *was* going to fight him on her own turf. She just wished she knew how.

Climbing on behind Colt, Lauren settled herself comfortably against him and held on to his waist. He touched her hands tenderly before starting the bike and leaving the park.

She thought more about his words. What could have caused him to lose hope, to lose his will to live? Her heart ached for him.

She wished she could help him in some way—could give him back his will to love and fight for life. It might just give them a future together—something she wished for desperately.

She sighed against his back. So many wishes, she thought. Would they ever come true?

By the time they reached the inn, more clouds had gathered. Unless it blew over, they would witness another spring thunderstorm before nightfall.

Colt parked the motorcycle right up in Lauren's front yard, near the steps. "Do you mind if I push this up onto your front porch?" he asked when she'd climbed off.

"No," she replied, wondering what made him think she could refuse him anything.

He climbed off, too, and moved to push the bike up the front steps of her porch.

"Colt," she said softly, and reached out to touch him, wanting to give him some comfort. She knew her touch couldn't take away whatever pain he held inside, but it was all she had to give him.

He pushed the bike away, moving out of her reach, just as her hand was about to make contact with his shoulder blade.

She pulled it back quickly, before he had the chance to see her standing that way.

"Colt," she said, when he had parked the bike. "About what you said before—"

"Forget it," he said sharply, stopping.

"But I can't forget it," she replied softly. "Why does it bother you so much that you had to shoot him? He was a criminal, robbing a bank, for crying out loud."

"Lauren," he said, his own voice growing softer to match her tone, "I'm not bothered at all that I had to shoot him. I only regret that I didn't do it sooner. And we don't have time to talk about any of this right now. I want to check out the inn, and I want you right beside me the whole time. We can continue this conversation later, if you think it's necessary. Besides, haven't you noticed anything?''

Lauren glanced around, trying to see just what she must have missed. Then it hit her like a blow to the stomach. "It's quiet," she whispered.

"Yes. Too damned quiet. Come on."

She climbed up the porch steps and came to stand beside him. He took his gun out with one hand and gave her hand a squeeze with the other. He placed a light, soft kiss of encouragement on her cheek.

Still standing near the motorcycle, he pulled out the rifle and handed it to her. Then he took out the knife—it was still wrapped in his handkerchief—but, much to her relief, he kept it.

"Is there anyone around here?" he asked.

"Pete, my handyman. His truck is still here." Lauren shrugged. "But he could be anywhere. Out checking the trails or fixing part of the fence. Doing anything. I don't see him every day."

"Stay with me."

She smiled. "It's the safest place I know."

The front door was slightly ajar, and Colt kicked it open the rest of the way. From the doorway, they could see most of the living room, down the hall into the kitchen, the bottom of the stairs, and into the dining room. And everything they saw was quiet and still.

Colt took a step into the building. Taking a hard, painful swallow, Lauren followed.

"Lock the door," Colt said, his voice incredibly loud in the silence.

"But what if he's already in here?" Lauren argued.

"If he's already in here, then we'll have no choice but to fight him. But we don't want him walking in behind us."

Lauren switched the rifle from one hand to the other, only to find both hands were shaking. Her heart pounding, she closed the door and turned the lock. The bolt snapped into place. Licking her lips and trying unsuccessfully to bring moisture to her dry mouth, she turned back to Colt.

Slowly they moved into the kitchen. The back door was still locked from when Lauren had latched it earlier, during her first encounter with Dillon Waters. She found it hard to believe it had happened less than twenty-four hours before. She stood just inside the doorway while Colt checked the lock to make sure it was secure. Broken glass from the plates still on the floor crunched beneath his feet.

At the sink, he rinsed the blood from his handkerchief and the knife. With the visible evidence washed down the drain, he put the knife into the dishwasher. When he had finished, he turned to her again and reached out to take the rifle from her hand. His fingers touched hers at the same time he met her gaze. The look in his eyes caused her to shiver, despite the afternoon heat.

"Stay behind me," he said. His husky words echoed through the empty, silent kitchen.

She could only nod.

Seconds turned into minutes. And the minutes turned into hours. Slowly, carefully, they searched the inn, checking every room, looking behind every piece of furniture, in every closet, behind every door, closing and locking all the windows as they passed.

Lauren stayed right behind Colt, looking for any sign of Dillon Waters, listening for any sign of movement in the house. In the dining room, she wiped up the pool of dried blood and cleaned the smeared print from the window.

"Well, he's not here," Colt said when they had returned to the kitchen. "Is there anyplace else he could be?"

Lauren had grabbed the broom from the closet and was absently sweeping up the broken plates out of the walkway. At his question, her gaze shifted to the closed basement door, her throat tightening with dread. "The basement," she whispered painfully.

Colt looked over at the closed door. "What's down there?"

Lauren shrugged. "The furnace. Some boxes and stuff." *And a lot of dark corners,* she nearly added.

Colt didn't seem to notice her apprehension. "Well, let's check it out."

He was at the door and nearly had it open before she was able to stop him. "Wait!" she said.

"What?"

"It's just that—" she began, suddenly feeling foolish.

"What?" he asked again.

"I just think that if he is in here, the basement would be the perfect place to hide," she said quickly.

"Do you want to stay up here?" he asked gently.

The tenderness of his voice almost brought tears to her eyes. She blinked them away, absolutely refusing to let them fall. The fact that he would venture down into that creepy dungeon all by himself revealed his caring and his concern for her. But she didn't want it now, not like this. She didn't want him risking his life for her. She loved him.

The realization was nearly her undoing. She didn't want Colt here just to help her fight Dillon Waters. She wanted him here for her. But with that realization, all the questions surrounding Colt returned. And she wondered if he'd ever be able to open himself up to her and let her inside him. She could only hope.

But first they had to get through the basement.

"No," she lied. "I'd rather go down there with you."

"All right, then, let's get this over with."

He turned the knob and slowly opened the door.

Lauren held her breath, certain that Dillon Waters was going to come jumping out at them. But only darkness and a musty, damp smell came up to meet them.

"Where's the light?" Colt asked.

"At the bottom of the stairs. There's a bulb hanging from the ceiling," Lauren replied. "You've got to pull the string."

"We have to walk down those stairs in the dark?" he asked.

"I have a flashlight," she said, taking it from a nearby kitchen drawer.

He looked toward the basement steps. "Fine. You hold it. I'll go first." That was fine with Lauren.

He set the rifle down beside the doorframe. "I'm leaving this here."

"But what if he's down there?"

"Listen, it's dark down there, and anything could happen. If one of us trips or sees a spider or something, it could go off accidentally. One of us could get hurt or even killed. And that would make it too easy for Waters. Does this door have a lock on it?" Colt asked.

"Yes."

The look he gave her was intense. "If anything happens, Lauren—anything—you run back up here and lock it."

"But I'd be locking you in." Lauren's heart was racing with fear at the thought of having to do as he asked. Though his concern for her touched her, she shook her head. Feeling as she did about him, she could never leave him. He hadn't left her alone, and she loved him too much to leave him, no matter what happened.

"Promise me you'll do it, Lauren." His glittering eyes held her gaze.

"I—"

"Promise me!"

"All right, I promise!" she finally said, hating herself for saying it, and hoping with all her being that it wouldn't come to that.

Silently, Colt slipped through the doorway. She wanted to tell him she loved him, just so that he knew, just in case something did happen, but he didn't give her the chance. And she had no choice but to follow him or be left alone.

Once on the basement stairs, the musty odor assaulted her. She could see Colt's back silhouetted against the darkness ahead of her. He was already two or three steps below her.

"Where's the light, Lauren?" he asked, his whispered voice sounding raspy.

She flipped on the flashlight and shone it down the stairs ahead of him. The small glow did little more than light the two steps ahead of him. He took another step down.

"The railing's broken," he whispered.

Lauren moved the light, and then she gasped, seeing the single-pole railing was broken in half. One end of it rested on the steps and the other hung over the side of the staircase.

Colt looked up at her. "I take it it wasn't always like this."

"No," she said.

She followed him down another step, and the boards beneath her creaked loudly under her weight. She wanted to reach out to him, to touch him and feel his warmth, to let him be her anchor in this dark sea of fear. But she forced herself to keep her hands to herself. She didn't want to distract him, no matter how much she wanted to touch him.

Colt moved like a cat—soundless, perfectly balanced, ready for anything. He'd reached the bottom of the stairs by the time Lauren had taken two more steps. Lauren shone the light on the ceiling so that he could see the string he had to pull to turn on the light.

Colt was reaching for the string when something closed around Lauren's ankle. Through her jeans, she felt the strength of fingers, of a hand. The sudden touch caused her to jump and drop the flashlight.

She cried out in alarm, and thought for certain that her heart was about to burst from fear. The hand closed more securely around her ankle and held on.

Feeling herself start to fall, she grabbed for the rail—it was no longer there. Suddenly, Colt's strong arms came out to grab her. He shoved her backward to keep her from falling headfirst down the few remaining stairs. She landed safely on the seat of her pants.

But the hand still held her ankle, and she began to kick out. Then, through the yellow glow of the ceiling light, she saw that it was Pete she was about to kick.

The handyman was lying on the floor. He'd reached up over the steps to grab her in order to get her attention. His face was a mass of bruises, and his nose was bleeding. "F-fell," he stammered. "Fell down the stairs."

"Oh, my gosh, Pete," Lauren said, her voice breathy with astonishment. She slipped out of his grasp and went down the last few stairs to the bottom, where she ran around to the older man.

Pete turned to face her and tried to speak, but he winced in pain. His lips moved soundlessly.

"Shh, don't try to speak. We'll get help for you. Just lie still," Lauren said softly. She knelt down beside him, and drew his head onto her lap, trying to see the extent of his injuries. "We need to call an ambulance, Colt," she added.

"As soon as I finish looking around down here" was his reply.

"But, Colt..." Lauren began, her voice rising with a flush of frustrated anger. Pete was hurt. Surely Dillon Waters wouldn't still be hiding down in the basement. Pete wasn't unconscious. He'd surely warn them if Dillon Waters was still around.

Unless...

Suddenly Lauren realized what was happening. It had been the same with Mav. She had reacted without thinking when she saw her injured pet. Now she was doing the same with Pete.

She looked down at Pete's bleeding face. She offered him a brave smile. "Hang on, Pete. We'll be able to get you help in just a few minutes." Her eyes moved to Colt, watching as he cautiously moved about the shadowed basement.

He searched every corner. He moved around boxes and checked out the old coal bin, which had been empty for years.

Much to Lauren's relief, it was empty still. Her heart pounded against her chest when Colt slowly moved around to the other side of the furnace and out of sight. The few seconds she couldn't see him felt more like hours, and she absently rubbed her chest when he reappeared. She wondered just how much more terror her heart could take. How ironic it would be if she ended up dying of a massive coronary after fighting Dillon Waters's attempts to end her life.

"It's all clear down here," said Colt, coming back to kneel down beside Lauren and Pete. "Do you want to stay with him or go up and call the ambulance?"

Lauren had no desire to stay in the basement any longer than was necessary. But Pete seemed to be so comfortable, leaning on her, and she hated to disturb him in any way.

"I'll stay," she said softly.

Colt's gaze held hers for a long moment. Lauren had the strangest feeling that he could see the fear she was trying to hide, and that he was trying to pass to her a bit of his own courage.

"I'll be right back," he said. Then he was gone, up the stairs and into the kitchen.

Lauren could hear him above her. First his footsteps on the kitchen floor. Then the sound of his muffled voice as he requested an ambulance.

She tried to concentrate on the sounds of his actions so that she wouldn't have to think about being in the basement without him. She looked down at Pete. He'd been a loyal employee and friend for years. She trusted him, and she'd see to it that he got the best of care.

When Colt came back down the stairs a few moments later, she let out a breath, only then realizing that she'd been holding it.

"Pete, what were you doing down here?" she asked softly, when the man opened his eyes.

"Well, I came to look for you. I saw those broken dishes, and there was no sign of you. I was going to call the police, but I thought I'd better check around here first." His deep voice was laced with the pain he must be feeling.

"Why were you looking for me in the first place?"

"I wanted to ask you if you had my sledgehammer. I couldn't find it anywhere."

Lauren looked up at Colt and did her best to mask the sudden panic that twisted around her heart at the realization that Dillon had probably used her sledgehammer to destroy those headstones.

"The ambulance is on its way," said Colt. His voice was soft, husky.

Lauren felt her expression soften, and she smiled at him, grateful for the change of subject. She just didn't have the strength to worry about the hammer. Knowing her luck with Dillon Waters, he'd probably left it where it would be conveniently found by the police. With her name painted on it, of course.

"How'd you fall down the steps, Pete?" Colt asked.

Pete's breathing was loud and raspy. "It was the strangest thing. At first I thought someone pushed me. But I'd just looked through the kitchen, and there wasn't anyone there."

"Just rest now, Pete," Lauren said, placing her hand against his cheek in a gentle, caring caress. "Just rest."

She looked up again at Colt. "Maybe we should call the police, too. Maybe they could check things out. If they found any evidence that someone else was in here and pushed Pete, it might help us.''

A loud banging from upstairs caught their attention. Then a muffled voice drifted down to them. ''Miss Baker, open the door! This is the police!''

Colt's gaze held hers. ''Sounds like we don't have to call them after all.''

CHAPTER TWELVE

"Go up and let them in, Lauren," Colt said.

Lauren hesitated, her gaze shifting to her injured friend. "But Pete—"

"I'll stay with Pete. Let the police in and bring them down here. Tell them we've already called an ambulance."

Reluctantly, Lauren shifted, letting go of Pete and moving away. Colt's gaze held hers as he moved to take her place next to Pete. "And Lauren?"

She turned back to him. "Yes?"

"Take off the gun."

"What should I do with it?"

He shrugged slightly. More knocking echoed down from the door upstairs. "I don't care. Put it in a kitchen drawer on your way through." He watched her go, his gaze never leaving her until she disappeared at the top of the stairs.

He looked down at the older man. "Pete—" Colt spoke softly "—don't say anything to the police about not being able to find your sledgehammer."

Pete's expression narrowed with evident confusion. "Who are you?" he whispered.

"Colt Norbrook," he replied. "There's someone who wants to hurt Lauren, and I'm here to help her. I think he probably used your hammer to commit a crime, hoping that the police would think Lauren did it. He really intends to hurt her, and I'm trying to stop him."

The sounds of footsteps and voices grew louder. The police were in the kitchen, above him.

"But Miss Baker's a nice lady. Why would someone want to hurt her?" Pete asked.

"I don't know, but I'm going to find out."

The sounds were at the basement door.

"Just keep her safe," Pete pleaded. "Just keep her safe."

Colt looked down at him. And a question swirled through his mind like a strong gust of wind. Could he keep her safe? Did he even have a chance? He'd been too late when it came to stopping Dillon Waters before, and an innocent victim had lost her life. It could happen again, and this time it would be Lauren who Colt would lose forever. And if that happened, he'd have lost everything.

He realized suddenly, his heart racing through his chest, that he'd sent her upstairs alone to open the door. He shook his head, listening intently to the muffled voices drifting down from the kitchen. He was still underestimating Waters. What if he was dressed in a police uniform or could change his appearance? What if he could control the police as he had controlled Lauren? Why had he let her go up alone?

The only way to protect Lauren was to stay with her every moment. She trusted him, just as that young hostage had. And he'd be damned if he was going to let Waters do anything like that again. He couldn't let Lauren down. He just couldn't.

Lauren came down the stairs followed by two policeman wearing blue uniforms. Colt said a silent prayer of thanks that neither of them looked like Dillon Waters.

Lauren quickly introduced them to Colt and Pete. "This is Officers Benton and McGillin."

"Mr. Galen takes care of your horses and works as sort of a handyman around here?" Officer Benton asked as he bent to inspect Pete's injuries.

"Yes," Lauren replied.

"Did you witness his fall down the stairs?"

And so began the line of questions, regarding where Lauren had been and what she had done in the past twenty-four hours.

"I was with Colt," she replied simply.

"You spent the night with him?"

"Yes," she replied without hesitation.

"I suppose you can verify that," said Officer Benton, looking at Colt.

Colt's gaze never wavered. "Yes, I can. She was with me at my cabin out on Willow Creek Road."

"We noticed glass on the floor upstairs."

"A few of my plates got broken," Lauren explained.

"How?"

"I dropped them, unloading the dishwasher," Lauren said.

"When?"

"Yesterday."

Benton's eyes narrowed, and McGillin simply stared at Lauren. "And you never cleaned it up?"

"I got called outside. And then Colt came, and I sort of forgot about it." Lauren couldn't tell if they believed her. Her lies felt as though they were all caught in her throat, choking her. She tried to look at Colt lovingly as though he always caused her to forget things.

"Ever visit the Holly Hill Cemetery?" Benton asked Colt, getting back to business and ignoring Lauren's look.

"No," Colt replied.

"What about you, Miss Baker?"

"No. I don't know anyone buried there. I'm not even sure if I know where it's located."

Benton stared at her. Colt recognized the old police trick of staring someone down in the hope of getting a few more answers. Thankfully, Lauren held his gaze and her tongue.

"Mr. Galen, if you're up to answering, how did you fall down the steps?"

Pete seemed to be growing weaker, and he was obviously in a great deal of pain as he tried to shift so that he could look right at the officer. "It was dark," he said softly. "And my balance isn't as good as it used to be when I was younger."

The distant sound of an approaching siren filtered down to them. "That sounds like the ambulance," said Colt.

"I'll go show them the way down here," Officer McGillin volunteered, speaking for the first time.

A few minutes later, Colt and Lauren watched as the ambulance attendants put Pete onto a gurney and brought him outside to the waiting ambulance.

"I'll come to the hospital as soon as I can, Pete," Lauren told him, giving him a gentle touch through the blanket that covered him.

Pete brought his hand out from under the blanket and grasped hers. "You stay with him," he whispered to her, his gaze moving to Colt. "He'll keep you safe. I know he will."

Lauren didn't get a chance to reply. The attendants slid Pete's gurney into the ambulance and one of them climbed in behind him. From his seat, one of the paramedics looked back at Lauren. "Perhaps you should come along and get checked out, miss. You don't look well."

Before Lauren could reply, Officer McGillin added, "He's right, Ms. Baker. You do look a bit under the weather. I could ride along with you and take down anything more you have to say."

Weakly Pete raised his head to look at Lauren. "Stay," he mouthed.

His single word left her wondering if he knew something about Dillon Waters or if this was all one of Dillon Waters's tricks.

It didn't matter. This was her home. She didn't plan to leave it and go to the hospital as a patient if she could help it.

"Thanks, but I'll stay," she replied, letting them close the ambulance door.

Within seconds, the ambulance was speeding away, leaving Colt and Lauren with the two waiting policemen and many more questions.

Lauren's headache grew with each one until she was forced to take more aspirin.

Inside the inn, the questioning went on for over an hour. The police explained that the Holly Hill Cemetery had been vandalized, but they didn't say to what extent.

"Ms. Baker, your name was painted on one of the headstones," explained Benton.

Lauren acted as surprised as possible. "My name? Are you sure it was my name? Why would someone do that? Surely, you don't think I would do something like that, do you?'' She pointed outside, to her flower bed. ''I was working out there until late yesterday afternoon. I'll have a full house Memorial Day weekend, Officer, and I'm trying to be ready for it. Besides, do you think I'm stupid enough to sign my own name to a crime so that you could catch me?''

Colt wasn't sure whether Officer Benton bought that or not. McGillin did, but it was clear to see he'd buy just about anything. Colt was reminded of the earlier statement he'd made to Lauren about how anyone who made it through the police academy had to have common sense. Looking at McGillin, he realized that perhaps he'd been wrong.

Benton moved his line of questioning back to the dishes on the kitchen floor and how they had gotten broken. Lauren kept to her story about having dropped them while unloading the dishwasher.

''Do you have destructive tendencies?'' Benton asked her.

''Of course not,'' she replied, knowing full well he was trying to tie her into the vandalism at the cemetery.

When it came to the question of why there was a loaded rifle in the kitchen, Colt told the officer it was his. He stressed the fact that Lauren had hired him to find out who was harassing her and that he felt this person was indeed dangerous. He was merely taking precautions, he told them. He even pointed out that she'd been to the police for help.

''Do you think perhaps this man who has been *harassing* you was in your house?'' Benton asked, his tone indicating that he really didn't believe anyone was bothering her. ''Perhaps, you should come down to the station and file a complaint.''

Lauren met his hard gaze. ''I've already done that.''

After seeing the permits that allowed Colt to carry weapons, Benton and McGillin left reluctantly. Their meager investigation had turned up no evidence that Dillon Waters had been in the house.

By the time he and Lauren ushered the two officers out the front door, Colt's insides were shaking with anticipation. He stood at the front door close to Lauren and watched the police drive off in their squad car. Lauren sighed heavily, and he took her hand.

"They never even said anything about the caretaker," said Lauren softly.

"That's because they were hoping one of us would slip and say something about it. Every investigation is done that way. Certain details aren't revealed to anyone, at least not at first, so that when there is a suspect or a confession, the police know that they have the right person." He placed a gentle arm around her and led her back inside. The low rumble of approaching thunder followed them in.

"I wonder if they even found the hammer." Lauren looked up at him. Her green eyes were sparkling, shining so brightly that for a moment Colt couldn't reply. He simply stared down at her.

"They probably haven't, or they would have questioned you about it, perhaps even arrested you if they felt it necessary. Did the hammer have anything on it that would tell them that it's yours? Any initials or anything?" he asked.

Lauren considered his question for a moment. "No, I don't think so. I didn't even really realize I owned a sledgehammer until today. What if Dillon Waters did something to show them it was mine?" she asked.

Colt pulled her close. "I don't know, but try not to worry about it. If the police do have the hammer, they haven't linked it to you or I'm sure we would have known."

"I'd love to take a shower," Lauren said, leaning over and resting her head against his shoulder.

Colt held her to him, reluctant to let her go. "Do we need to check your horses first?" he asked.

"I guess we probably should."

"You could stay locked up in here and I could go," he offered, even though leaving her alone was not something he really wanted to do.

His concern with keeping her safe, and his willingness to risk his own life for her, touched Lauren's heart. "No, I'll go with you," she said. "I'll take a shower when we're finished."

Colt smiled. "Then get your keys and we'll lock everything up."

The stable was quiet except for the soft rustling sounds of the horses' subtle movements. They checked the building out just as they had the house. Slowly, guns held at the ready, they moved from stall to stall, checking every corner. There was no sign of Dillon Waters.

"Maybe I finally convinced him I don't love him, and he's decided to leave me alone," Lauren stated hopefully.

"Maybe," muttered Colt. He tried to sound as hopeful as she did, but he knew better. He knew Dillon Waters was a conniving liar. Even if he came forward and said he'd never bother Lauren again, Colt wouldn't believe him. Looking closely at Lauren, he could see why Dillon would love her. She was beautiful. She *was* everything a man could want in a woman. It would be difficult *not* to fall for her. And yet one question continued to plague him. "How did he come to love you so much, Lauren, if you don't know him?"

She was standing at the first stall, petting a white mare. "I don't know. But his claim sounds genuine. When he grabbed me that first time, he had a firm grip, and I couldn't get away. And yet, at the same time, it was almost like a caress. It was loving and gentle. It was so strange, so contradictory. And I remember other things, like bits and pieces that he's said, and his love seems real. It just doesn't make sense why he'd want to kill me because of it."

"He doesn't want anyone else to have you," Colt said simply. *Especially me,* he nearly added.

What a reason, Lauren thought, turning her attention back to the mare.

They fed and watered the horses, and Lauren told him about each one.

Snowflake, her white mare, was her prize. "I'm sorry I didn't get to ride you today, girl," she said to the animal, feeding her oats out of her hand. Lauren petted her fine coat, her love for the animal evident in her every gesture.

In the next stall was a black stallion. "This is Lightning," she said.

"Why Lightning?" Colt asked. "Does he run as fast as lightning?"

Lauren laughed. It was a genuine sound, soft and rippling, and Colt's heart caught. This was the first time he'd ever heard her laugh, and it was a sound he wanted to hear again and again.

"I don't know if he can run like lightning," she admitted, still smiling. "I only know he hits trees like lightning. He also hits fenceposts and the corners of the stable. The poor guy must be nearsighted because as soon as he gets started he runs into something." She rubbed the stallion gently. "But he's great around people, and nothing seems to frighten him. So even though we never send him out on the trails we sometimes harness him up to the tree right outside so the children can ride him around in a circle."

They finished in the stable, taking care of all the other horses, and made their way back into the house just as the first raindrops touched down.

"I guess if I still want to take a shower, I can always just stand out there," Lauren joked, closing and locking the door behind them.

Colt chuckled softly. "It's good to hear happiness in your voice instead of fear," he said.

The rain was coming down harder. He could hear it hitting the porch roof.

She offered him a small smile. "Sometimes it's easier to pretend things are normal. Like when I'm out there with my horses, life feels so right. Then, after a few moments, my head hurts again and I don't feel very well. It's almost as if my headache is there to remind me that someone wants to kill me."

He gently pulled her into his embrace. Her soft woman's scent filled his senses. This woman in his arms continued to show him so many different sides of herself. There was the fragile side, the delicate side that he saw right now. Then there were the strong, courageous side, the confident side, the fighting side and the uncertain side. Last night, when she'd taken the bed sheet with her into the bathroom, he'd seen the modest, almost bashful side of her. And just before that, he'd not only seen, but felt her passionate side.

He wanted to protect all of her. She was so changed from that first time he'd seen her. He remembered that day in the grocery store, when their carts had collided. The rosiness of her skin, combined with her fiery hair and eyes that sparkled like emeralds, had captured his attention. He'd stuttered an apology, unable to remember the last time he'd been nearly speechless upon seeing a woman. In a single instant, he'd been captured by her looks. In the next, he'd been captured by her smile, a radiant, warm, glowing smile that settled somewhere deep inside him.

Now her skin was pale except for the circles beneath her eyes which were becoming darker and darker. Griff Waters, Officer McGillin and one of the ambulance attendants had all noticed that she didn't look well. It could simply be the flu. Then again, maybe Dillon Waters had infected her with something strong enough to kill her. Either way, he decided, he was taking her to see a doctor. Not to the hospital. She'd fight him all the way if he tried to get her to the hospital. It would have to be a private doctor. Yes, he would take her to Dr. Bridgeton's office in Rock Hill.

That decided, he placed a soft kiss on her brow. "Why don't you take your shower down here, while I fix you something to eat? It seems as though with all the excitement we missed lunch," he said quietly. His lips brushed against the softness of her hair. The touch triggered a response deep inside him that he hadn't expected. And with that response came the growing, smoldering heat of wanting more.

Memories washed over him. Memories of their lovemaking the night before. Memories of the way she'd felt and the passion that she'd given him. Momentarily he closed his eyes against the heat that soared through him from those memories. He wanted to ignore the fact that she obviously didn't feel well, that she needed to eat. He wanted to ignore everything, so that he could ease her right down to the wood floor and make love to her. He wanted her now, in the daylight, so that he could see every part of her he touched and tasted.

"That sounds like a wonderful idea," she replied, breaking into his thoughts. And for a moment he thought she was referring to the idea of making love on the floor. "Unless, of course, everything you cook tastes as bad as the bacon and eggs you made for breakfast."

He groaned inwardly and let go her. His arms felt empty without her, but it was the only way he could ease some of the burning heat that she brought to him. "You'll love it, I promise," he said through a tight throat.

He led her to the bathroom and looked in, checking to make sure nothing and no one had crept in while their backs were turned. The window was securely locked.

All was in order, and yet he was still reluctant to leave her. It wasn't that he wanted to stand and watch her shower like some sick individual—he wanted to climb into the shower with her. He wanted to soap her down and feel every single inch of her. The wanting threatened to consume him. He swallowed hard, working to fight it, to at least control it.

"I'll be in the kitchen if you need anything," he muttered.

Stepping out of the bathroom, he pulled the door closed. He leaned against it, sucking in deep breaths, trying to stop the fire raging through him.

Just when he thought there was some hope of control, the bathroom door opened from the other side, and he fell in against her. He tried to protect her and stop himself from falling at the same time, but the action had come too quickly, too suddenly, too unexpectedly. One moment he was leaning against the door, and the next he found himself on the floor on top of Lauren.

Well, this is one way to get her on the floor, he thought. Then looking into her eyes, seeing her shock, seeing her unhealthy-looking complexion, he hated himself for thinking such things. Trying not to hurt her, he moved to climb off her and stand up. His knee slipped right between her thighs, and he closed his eyes, trying to ignore the rush of heat that pulsed up his leg.

He moved to put his hand on the floor and push himself up, away from her. But she shifted at the same time, and his palm grazed her breast, sending an even more intense surge of heat up his arm.

"Lauren..." he ground out, gritting his teeth. He was trying so hard to ignore what he wanted and do what was right for her.

For a moment he thought he just might succeed in doing the right thing. Then Lauren reached up and gently placed her hand on his cheek.

The warmth of her touch sent something close to a bolt of lightning through him. And, to his amazement, thunder crashed close by outside.

She looked up at him, her green eyes sparkling. And she grinned.

The lucid look in her eyes, mixed with her subtle grin, was enough to snap what little control he had left. He leaned down and covered her lips with his own, letting the heat of her fill him, letting it take over and burn away any fears and doubts that might be lingering.

Her tongue came into his mouth, and Colt thought he would surely burn up. He pulled away from her suddenly, thinking that if he didn't, the two of them would burn together.

Her gaze caught his, and she smiled at him wickedly. Then she laughed. It was a deep, throaty chuckle that kept the heat building in him.

"What?" he asked, still trying to catch his breath.

"This morning I promised myself I wouldn't let this happen again," she replied, her voice deep and husky with passion.

Colt forced himself to swallow and wait. "And now?"

"I can't keep the promise," she said. "I can't even begin to control this." She pushed her hips against him. "How is it that it's so strong between us?"

"I don't know," he answered honestly. Thoughts of his grandfather flashed through his mind, and he remembered the words the old man had spoken regarding Colt's destiny. Was this his destiny? Was this the fire the old man had mentioned?

Lauren broke into his thoughts. "It's so much more than just sex. It's you. It's wanting you, all of you, and only you."

"I know," he told her.

"Then you feel it, too? You feel the strength of it?"

Oh, he felt it, all right. "Yes." His whispered reply was harsh as he forced the word through his tight, burning throat.

"Then take a shower with me," she said, invitingly.

He released a sound that was part sigh, part groan. "I thought you'd never ask."

CHAPTER THIRTEEN

Thunder cracked loudly somewhere above them, and Colt wasn't sure if it had touched down in the room with them or if it was still outside. Perhaps it was even inside his body.

He was certain of one thing—Lauren beneath him, feeling hot, her need reflecting his. She tore his shirt open and placed her palms on his chest. Her touch burned his flesh. She moved her hands up to cup his face and pulled him down to her to capture his lips in another soul-searing kiss.

He didn't want it like this. He didn't want it hot and fast. He wanted to savor every touch, every moment. He wanted his senses to revel in every single aspect of her, of what he would give to her and take from her.

Tearing his mouth from hers, he moved his lips gently to kiss her jaw. He forced himself to move slowly on to the soft, tender flesh of her throat. "I thought you wanted to take a shower," he murmured.

"Later. Right now, I don't want you to stop. Not for anything. You make it wonderful. You make me so alive. You make everything so real, so vivid, so wonderfully alive," she said, her voice breathy and warm in his ear. "You make me forget everything but you." She ran her fingers through his hair before sliding them slowly down his back and around to the front of his pants. In the next instant, she was unbuckling his belt and working at the button of his jeans.

He undid the buttons of the shirt she wore, slowly, carefully, concentrating on keeping his fingers from ripping it apart. It was his shirt, and yet at the same time it was also her shirt. He'd meant what he said about wanting to see her wear it after he made love with her. He wanted to see her in it so often that it would eventually fall apart from wear, from her putting it on and his taking it off again.

He opened the shirt to reveal her breasts. He admired their beauty for a brief moment before putting his hand on one and his mouth on the other. She moaned and pushed against him, her pelvis rocking against him in an explosive movement.

Despite his desire to take it slow, he couldn't wait any longer. He needed her. He needed to possess her in the deepest, most intimate way, and he needed it now. Next time, he promised himself. Next time, he'd take it slow.

He struggled out of his jeans as she kicked out of hers. In the next instant, he was part of her. Fully. Completely.

"Colt..."

At the sound of her voice, he pushed into her harder.

He looked down and saw that her cheeks were now filled with color. She was warm, flushed and rosy, and more beautiful than he'd ever seen her. Her eyes sparkled with hot green fire, and her hair fanned out around her face. Her lips were red and swollen from his kisses. He never wanted to stop looking at her. He never wanted to stop loving her.

She grasped him and pulled him down to her so that his entire body pressed against hers, his flesh covering hers. She drew her arms around his neck and shoulders and wrapped her legs around his waist. "I need you," she whispered. "I need you. I need you." She whispered it over and over. She held him so tight her nails dug into his back and his shoulders.

"Harder," she said, her voice harsh in his ear.

"How's this?" he asked, accommodating her.

"Yes."

"But I can't hold on any longer," he bit out.

She smiled up at him, her eyes twinkling. "Then just hold on to me and let everything else go."

She brought her lips back to his. The impact was all either of them needed. Holding on to one another, they let go of the world and tumbled over the edge of reality, far beyond the point of return.

Colt closed his eyes, letting his raw release sweep through him. Then he heard pounding, and after a moment realized it was his own heart, beating in unison with hers.

"Lauren?" He opened his eyes and looked down at her, but her own eyes were closed. She appeared to be asleep and her face was once more a pale, pastelike color.

"Lauren?" he said again, louder now, his grip on her arms tightening.

Her eyes opened in an instant. "What?"

"Are you ready for your shower?" he asked, slowly, trying to bring his breathing under some sort of control.

"Yes," she replied, giving him a little smile. "You're coming in with me, aren't you?"

"I wouldn't miss it for anything." He helped her up and into the shower stall.

Under the warm spray, he rubbed soap over every inch of her. All the while, he studied her, admired her, and kissed her again and again. He slowly massaged her scalp while he washed her hair, gently running his fingers through it, then tipping her head back under the spray to rinse it.

"You have great hands," she said softly. "So strong, so gentle."

"And you have a beautiful body, lush and full in just the right places." He brushed his palms over her soapy breasts as he spoke. "I want to make love to you again and again. Here. Now. I want to love you over and over."

She stopped at his words and looked at him.

"What's the matter?" he asked.

With her wet hair pulled back, away from her face, she looked paler than she had before they made love. Her eyes were large and searching. "I want that, too," she said slowly.

He smiled down at her through the spray before bringing his lips to hers in a slow, wet kiss. The fire between them ignited again. Only this time, he succeeded in taking it slow, taking his time, relishing every touch.

The water had cooled when Colt finally got around to turning it off. Reaching out to grab a thick, plush towel, he wrapped it around her and used it to pull her close to him. She shivered and moved closer to him. She was looking up at him with such trust in her eyes that, for a moment, he forgot about drying her. For a moment, he forgot everything. For that single moment, his heart might even have ceased to function. He'd seen that look before. That girl in the bank, that innocent victim had looked at him just that way, and he had hoped never to see that look again—and especially not on Lauren's face.

He swallowed hard and pushed the feeling of unease and insecurity away. He wished like hell she'd never looked at him that way. He didn't know if he could live up to that trust.

Lauren leaned her head against his chest, and he couldn't see her eyes any longer.

"Are you all right?" he asked softly. "I didn't get too rough before, did I?"

Against his chest, she sighed. "No, I'm just tired."

It was almost completely dark when they finally emerged from the bathroom. Lauren was wearing only her fluffy terry robe, and Colt was again dressed in his jeans and bright shirt. They had also taken the time to freshen one another's bandages.

Once in the kitchen, Lauren braved a glance out the window. "Do you think he's out there, hiding in the dark?"

"Yes." Colt knew it would be stupid to underestimate Waters, and he wouldn't lie to Lauren about it.

"When are you going to tell me everything about him?" she asked quietly.

Colt turned and looked at her, his expression growing hard and dark.

He was going to put off telling her again, she just knew it. And she was tired of it. She was tired of his shutting her out, especially after what they had just shared. "I deserve to know," she insisted. When he still said nothing, she pushed further. "You can't just leave me hanging with that statement about shooting him. Tell me what happened. Please . . ." She closed her eyes for a long moment, her expression revealing her frustration. "I feel like he's playing these mind games with me, and I don't know what to do to get ahead of him. If you know things about him, it would really help me.

"Will you please tell me everything?" She was practically begging.

At first, he wasn't sure he could, especially with Lauren's eyes filled with such innocence and trust. But finally he nodded slowly. "Everything."

Colt directed her to a chair.

"What are you doing?" she asked.

"I will tell you everything, but first, I'm living up to my promise of fixing you something to eat."

"I can hardly wait," she muttered.

"Now how can I go wrong?" he asked, grinning. He held up a can that he'd retrieved from her pantry. "I have a perfect can of chicken noodle soup and I have a pan." He held that up, too. "I have a stove on which to heat it." He turned on the flame of a burner, as if to prove he knew how to work it. "And, last but not least, I have a spoon with which to stir it."

Lauren laughed.

"Now," he said, looking at her seriously, "if only I had a way to open the can."

Lauren laughed and gestured with her hand. "In that drawer."

Within minutes, the room was filled with the soup's aroma. It dispelled the dampness that had accompanied the ongoing rain.

"So are you going to tell me now?" she questioned him as he set a steaming bowl of soup in front of her.

He got his own bowl and put out bread and butter before he replied. "I've been trying to decide just where to start."

"Start at the beginning."

"That sounds so easy," he replied. "I first met Dillon Waters in a park in Glendale. That was where I used to live. I didn't know his name at the time, and I didn't learn it until months later. It was early, and I was jogging before I had to go in to work. Waters had snatched some woman's purse, and I, being a good cop, chased him." Colt absently stirred his soup. "I caught him and got the purse, but he hit me, just like he did yesterday, before I could get a hold on him. He got away."

Lauren was taking in his every word, and he noticed she hadn't even picked up her spoon. "How's your soup?" he asked, to remind her of it. He was hoping some hot food might bring back a bit of her color. He couldn't be sure, but he thought she looked even paler than before, and her skin seemed to have taken on a chalky tone.

He didn't continue until she took a bite. "It's good," she told him. "Then what?" Her hair was drying, becoming thousands of tiny waves the color of fire all over her head.

"So then," he went on, "a few months later, I meet up with him again. He tried to rob a convenience store, and I just happened to be in there buying a six-pack. I couldn't believe my dumb luck. And that time, I got him. Even though the workday was over for me, I arrested him and took him all the way down to the station and booked him." He paused, remembering the occasion as though it had happened yesterday. "You should have heard him. All the way down to the station, he called me every name in the book. He told me he was going to cut me into pieces the first chance he got. He said he knew where I lived, and he was going to find out where my family lived and go after all of them, too."

"And his father said he was such a good boy," Lauren put in.

Colt's eyes met hers across the table. "Do you know how hard it was for me not to tell him the truth this morning? I nearly did, and then I thought, why shatter the man's dreams of having a good son? I'm sure every parent wants to believe his kid is at least better than the parent, right?"

Lauren shrugged.

"There was one thing that Dillon said that day that was true," Colt said.

"What?"

"He told me he'd be back out on the streets in a matter of hours, and he was right. Despite a long list of arrests, he managed to get a judge in a good mood and a public defender who knew how to weasel her way around a courtroom, and he got out on bail. He even had a few so-called friends who helped him pay it."

He took a spoonful of his own soup, hoping she would follow suit and eat hers. Absently she did.

"He actually called me at my own apartment to tell me he was out and that I'd better watch my back or he was going to stick a knife in it."

"That sounds more like the Dillon Waters I know," Lauren put in.

"Then, about a week later, he tries to rob that bank. He's armed with enough firepower to start his own private war, and he's got a bankful of hostages to help him along the way. And somehow I have that same dumb luck. It turns out that my team gets assigned to bring him out and keep the hostages safe."

Colt was quiet for a long moment. The only sounds in the room were the falling rain outside and the sliding of his spoon against his bowl as he stirred his soup.

"You can't blame yourself for shooting him," Lauren said. "It was in the line of duty, right? You had to do it to save the hostages, right?"

His gaze met hers again. "Yes, it was in the line of duty, and as I said before, I don't blame myself for actually shooting him," he replied, his voice filled with sarcasm. "But I made a mistake that no cop should ever make. I did something that is almost worse than giving up my gun."

"What could possibly be so bad?" she asked.

The compassion in her voice touched him. "I underestimated him, and I hesitated. I knew him to be a robber and a thief but I didn't think he would kill anyone. And that was my mistake. I had my sights right on him when he grabbed a hostage, one of the tellers. She was so young. I hesitated for one single second and looked at her. I took my eyes off of Waters and looked at that girl. I saw her fear. I saw trust written all over her face. She trusted me to get her out of there safely." He thought of the look in the girl's eyes, the same look Lauren had given him just a short time before.

He let go of his spoon suddenly, and it clanked loudly against the side of his bowl.

"He killed her right there in front of me, in front of all the other hostages and half the police force. He shot her before I could shoot him. I know it sounds absurd, but I felt as if he only did it to get to me."

His throat was tight again. For the first time in months, the numbness brought on by the memory began to abate and his emotions took over. Frustration, rage and sadness were all rolled up into some kind of tight ball inside him. And that ball was rolling through him, growing in strength and size.

Lauren got up and came around the table to him. She leaned down and put her arms around him. "It wasn't your fault. You couldn't have known."

"Yes, it was. I didn't take the shot when I first had it. I had this crazy thought that I could outsmart him, that I could get him to simply walk out of the bank without hurting anyone. I failed."

"No, you did what you thought was right. He had a gun, and if you had shot him, it still could have gone off and killed someone."

He clung to her. Her touch was what he needed to ease the pain. Her closeness and her warmth were strong enough to push away some of the guilt. He remembered the way he'd thought Lauren was his second chance after he made love to her that first time, and now he knew it to be true. He had taken the job thinking he had to in order to keep Lauren from falling into Dillon Waters's hands. But he'd had no idea just how much taking the job would help his own life. Until now.

"I can't even tell you what I felt when I saw his picture in those newspaper clippings you brought me. There are no words to describe it," he said, his words muffled as he spoke against her. "I thought the whole world was coming crashing down on my head. And no matter how long or hard I looked at those pictures, I still didn't want to believe what I was seeing. I thought he'd come right out of my haunted dreams and into reality. In all my years on the police force, I can't remember ever feeling such terror. I was terrified for you. I thought of him trying to kill you, and I could hardly think rationally." He held her tighter, as though he could actually draw life from her.

For a long time, she simply held him, neither of them speaking, the room perfectly still except for the pounding of their hearts. When she finally, reluctantly, released him, he found that his soup was cold. So he warmed both bowls in her microwave.

"Dillon Waters said he fixed it so you could never love," she said. "I don't understand that."

The smile Colt offered her was filled with bitterness. "He said that, did he?" He didn't wait for her to reply before going on. "My shooting him—or my hesitation in shooting him, I should say—fixed a lot of things. I couldn't do my job right after that. I worried about everything, about every situation. I worried that I'd make another mistake that might cost someone's life. Every time I dated someone, I'd compare her to the girl that Waters killed. I dreamed of that girl, and in my dreams, she kept asking me why—why didn't I help her when I had the chance? It got to the point where I didn't want to sleep or eat. I was like a walking time bomb, and nobody wanted to work with me for fear that I had some sort of death wish and I'd take someone else along with me when the bomb went off."

"So what happened?" Lauren asked. She tried to envision him in such agony, and her heart twisted at the thought.

"Well, it's policy that after any shooting, the officer involved has to see a police psychologist. And mine suggested that I take a leave of absence. I followed his advice and took a leave—a permanent one."

She reached across the table and took his hand. He grasped hers in return, knowing that he must be crushing hers. And still he was unable to let her go.

"I sold the small amount of furniture I owned, put everything else in storage, got on my bike and started riding."

"And you just happened to stop here?" Lauren stated.

"No, there was more to it than that," he replied. "It was as if something was guiding me. I came here on purpose to see where he grew up, to find out if there was something here that caused him to be the criminal he was, something that would ease my mind and make him leave me alone."

"And did you find anything?"

"No. I found a beautiful place, an inviting place, but that's all. Then I found you. And I know you probably won't believe this, but I felt as if *you* were the real reason I was brought here."

"You said he called you?" Lauren asked. "What if he had this planned the whole time, to get you here so that you could help me, so that he could hurt you?" The thought was mind-boggling. "But then," she went on, "he just happened to see me and decided he wanted me."

Colt thought about her questions before shaking his head. "I don't think so," he said. "I think it goes much deeper than that."

"What if he somehow saw you bump into me in the store and knew how you wanted me, too, and he's just trying to kill me to get back at you?"

Now there was a question, he thought. What if Dillon had been able to get into his thoughts. He would have known just how much he had wanted Lauren from the first moment he saw her. Dear God, he thought. He stared at Lauren, knowing what he was going to have to do if that was true. He was going to have to give her up. If he wanted to save her at all, he would have to let her go. Dillon was just using her to get to him. He could see that now. But he couldn't let her die just because of a grudge Dillon had against *him*.

Lauren nervously bit her lower lip.

He'd seen her bite her lip like that before, when she was nervous or uncertain. The first time he'd seen her do it was at his office. He'd had to keep himself from staring, had to push aside any thoughts of kissing those rich, full lips.

And seeing her bite her lip now, he had the same reaction. If the table weren't between them, there'd be nothing to stop him from leaning close and tasting her again. He swallowed and tried to push the thought aside.

"I have to leave," he told her.

Her eyes widened, and he could see that she'd stopped breathing.

"What? Where? Why?"

"Don't you understand?" he attempted to explain. "You could be right. He may be using you to get to me."

"Yes, I do understand," she said simply.

"So, I've got to leave you. I can't let him use you anymore."

She chuckled bitterly. "And you think that's going to make him stop coming after me? I doubt it."

"Lauren—"

"And just how easy is that going to be for you to do?"

"Red—"

How could he call her that and think of leaving at the same time? she wondered. "We don't even know if you're the true reason he wants to kill me. You said yourself that we don't have a chance against him unless we work together," she argued.

"But that was before—"

"But nothing, Colt. You made me realize that I didn't want to face him alone, no matter what. Now you're saying you want to leave to save me. Well, I'm telling you, if you walk out now, whether he comes after me or not, I will never forgive you."

CHAPTER FOURTEEN

"And this spring storm pattern is expected to continue for the next two to three days."

The television weatherman was pointing to pictures of cloud patterns that had been taken from a satellite.

They'd finished their light meal and cleaned up their few dishes and were now seated in the living room, watching the news. Colt reclined comfortably on the sofa, his bare feet up on the coffee table, and Lauren was stretched out beside him, using his lap for a pillow. Tenderly he twisted her hair around his fingers while he took in the five-day forecast. He should have known he could never leave her. He glanced down at her, knowing now that whatever Dillon Waters's reasons were for wanting to kill her, to kill them both, they had to face it together. His heart gave him no choice in the matter. As long as there was breath in his body, he would not leave her.

"I'm afraid to go to sleep," Lauren said.

"Relax, Red," he told her softly. "We're ready for anything." He gave her cheek a gentle caress before moving his fingers back to her hair.

Lauren supposed they were ready. The rifle was leaning against the wall right next to the couch, and Colt had strapped on his holstered gun as soon as he dried off from his shower. Though Lauren hadn't put her gun on again, Colt had set it on the coffee table.

"Are the doors locked?" she asked, not caring about the forecast on the television, not caring whether it rained for the next forty days or not.

"Yes, everything's secure," he replied, offering her a little smile when he looked down at her. "How are you feeling?"

"Not too bad. I'm just a little tired, that's all. And my head still hurts a bit."

He moved his hand to the soft flesh of her throat. "Then you need to close your eyes and rest," he stated.

"I just know that if I do go to sleep, I'll wake up to find Dillon Waters here in some shape or form."

"I'm not moving, Lauren," he said softly. "I'm going to be right here, and you're going to stay right here with me. He's not getting past me. Nothing is going to happen. Together, we're not going to let anything happen."

"I hope you're right," she replied softly.

"Besides," he went on, "if Waters does come, I may just let him in. It's time to end this once and for all."

The thought of letting Dillon in caused Lauren to shiver.

"Cold?" Colt asked.

"Yes." It seemed as though the only time she could get warm now was when Colt made love to her.

There was a heavy cotton throw draped over the back of the couch, and Colt covered her with it. Gently he tucked it under her neck. "Better?"

"Yes, much," she replied, despite the fact that the throw did little good. Colt's hands were what warmed her. He must have read her mind, for he kept one arm draped across her and, through the cotton throw, held on to her arm.

An evening game show came on the television, and Colt let it play. The room filled with the sounds of the applauding audience and the spinning of a wheel.

Lauren finally gave in and closed her eyes. The darkness, mixed with the feel of Colt around her, was comforting, and within moments she drifted off.

Colt looked down and watched her sleep. He could spend every evening of his life just like this, with Lauren comfortably snuggled against him, and be very happy.

He just wished Lauren looked healthier. If he weren't aware of the way her chest rose and fell with her breathing, he'd almost think she was dead. Her pale face appeared almost ghostly, and the dark circles around her eyes gave them a sunken appearance.

Maybe he was making a mistake in waiting until the morning to take her to the doctor's office. What if tomorrow was too late? What if she simply slipped away from him in her sleep? It was evident she was sick with something. Dear God, he didn't want to think about losing her. She was his chance, she was his life.

A roar of thunder broke, as if to validate his thoughts. He had to get Lauren to a doctor, and he couldn't wait until morning.

He shifted slowly, so as to not wake her, and slipped out from under her. His movement brought nothing but a sleepy sigh as she settled on the couch without him.

In the kitchen, he searched the drawers until he found a telephone directory. Assuming that Dr. Bridgeton's office would be closed, he called the doctor's home number.

"Dr. Bridgeton?" he asked, when a male voice answered the phone.

"Yes?"

Colt took a deep breath and told the doctor who he was. "I have a patient, and I was wondering if you'd take a look at her. I don't think she's well."

"Can't this wait until tomorrow?"

"No...I don't think so."

There was a pause. "Well, if it's an emergency, she should be taken to a hospital."

"I can't do that, Doctor," Colt replied in his most authoritative voice.

The doctor didn't ask him to elaborate. Colt swallowed hard and waited.

"All right," said Dr. Bridgeton. "Can you have her at my office in twenty minutes?"

"Yes." The single word came out with a sigh of relief.

"I'll meet you there."

"Thank you, Doctor," Colt told the man before hanging up.

He moved to the kitchen window and stared out at the rain, telling himself over and over that he was doing the right thing. He was saving Lauren. Never mind that he would be forced to take her from the shelter of the house. He had no other choice.

A sudden burst of lightning lit up the sky, giving Colt a clear look at the yard. The sudden brilliance of it startled him.

But what startled him even more was the movement he saw, or thought he saw, just outside. He stepped closer to the window, trying to see through the darkness, which had just as quickly swallowed everything again.

He looked and waited, but there was nothing. And after a long moment of waiting, he finally turned and headed back to the living room to wake Lauren.

She jumped at his touch, instantly awake.

"What? What is it?" she asked, looking around.

Colt knew who she was expecting to find. "Relax," he said softly. "It's just me."

"Dillon Waters isn't here, is he?" she asked. Her eyes looked so large in her pale face.

"No, there's no sign of him." He paused. "I want to take you up to see Dr. Bridgeton."

She blinked at him. "Right now? What time is it? How long have I been asleep?"

"Not long," he replied, sitting down next to her. "And yes, I want to take you right now. He's agreed to see you, and he'll be in his office in twenty minutes." He grabbed her hand, and was shocked by how cold she felt to his touch. And he knew then that he was doing the right thing. She was slipping away right before his eyes. He had to do everything he could in order to stop it.

She glanced past him to the window and out at the storm. "I don't want to go out there. Dillon Waters could be hiding anywhere out there in the dark."

"We have to go, Lauren," he told her. "Anyone with eyes could see you're not well. And if you tell me you feel fine, I'll know you're lying."

"It's really nothing, Colt. It's probably just a bout of the flu. I'm sure I'll be fine by tomorrow."

The way she looked, he had the feeling that a lot of tomorrows were going to have to pass before she was fine again, but he didn't tell her that. He did, however, agree with her on one thing. "You are going to be fine, Red, because I'm going to make sure of it. Starting with a trip to see Dr. Bridgeton."

"But—"

"No more arguing," he said, interrupting. "I can tell you right now, you won't win. I'm taking you into Rock

Hill if I have to carry you out of here kicking and screaming. Now, you can put on some clothes or you can go wearing nothing more than the robe you've got on. Either way is fine by me. But you're going."

"All right," she said after a moment. "I'll just go upstairs and put on some jeans."

"I'm giving you three minutes," he said, thinking she was looking sicker by the minute.

He was standing at the bottom of the stairs, holding the cotton blanket in one hand and the flashlight they'd used before in the other, when she came back down, dressed in jeans and a sweatshirt. "Put this around you," he said. "We'll need to take your truck. I took the keys off the kitchen table where you left them."

"All right," she said softly. She reached for the blanket, and Colt handed her one end. Keeping the other end, he wrapped her in it.

He held her to him and looked down into her eyes for a moment that seemed to last a lifetime.

"Ready?" he asked.

"No," she replied honestly. "But I guess I have no choice, do I?"

"No." With one arm still around her, he led her to the door.

"Will you leave all the lights and the television on?" she asked.

"If you want. Why?" He looked at her, knowing she was stalling, knowing she didn't want to go out into the unknown. He didn't blame her. He didn't want to go, either.

"I don't want to come back to a dark, silent house," she replied.

"Can you carry this?" He handed his rifle to her.

"Yes." She took it, holding the blanket closed with one hand.

The air was cool and damp, and the sound of the falling rain grew instantly louder when Colt opened the door. He stepped out onto the porch first, alert and looking for anything out of the ordinary.

"Don't forget to lock it," Lauren said as she stepped out behind him.

Colt looked around for another moment before turning back to lock the dead bolt. When he was finished, he flipped on the flashlight and shone it beyond the edge of the porch.

The small beam of light reflected off the falling rain, revealing very little in the darkness. Colt pulled Lauren close again, and held one arm around her while he held the light in the other.

They encountered nothing but rain going to her truck, and after checking it with the light and finding nothing, Colt helped her in.

In the cab, she leaned close to him and shivered. He put his arm around her in an attempt to warm her with his own body heat.

The roads were slippery and almost impossible to see through the storm. Colt was forced to drive much slower than he anticipated, and he worried that Dr. Bridgeton wouldn't wait for them if they were late.

Much to his relief, a single car was parked in front of the Rock Hill Family Health Clinic. Through the large front door he could see the silhouette of a man in a white coat waiting near a counter. He led Lauren through the automatic door.

"Dr. Bridgeton?"

"Yes. You must be Colt Norbrook."

"Yes," replied Colt. "Is there any way we can lock that door so no one can get in?"

At his question, Dr. Bridgeton eyed Colt's gun cautiously. "I'm not sure that would be wise, Mr. Norbrook," he replied slowly.

With Lauren leaning against him, Colt quickly explained who and what he was, that Lauren's life was in danger and that she'd hired him to protect her. "Please," Colt said. "I'm not here for anything but to have you check her out." They'd left the rifle in the truck, and for the first time, Colt was glad of that. He had the feeling the doctor wouldn't believe a word of it if he saw all of Colt's firepower.

Dr. Bridgeton looked at Lauren for a long moment, analyzing her in the way only a member of the medical profession can. "What's your name?" he asked her.

"Lauren Baker."

"How long have you been feeling ill?"

"Since early this morning or late last night. I can't remember," she replied truthfully. It seemed to her that it had started just after Colt made love to her the night before, when she'd dreamed that Dillon Waters was trying to strangle her, but she couldn't be sure.

Dr. Bridgeton turned his attention to Colt. "All right, I'll lock that door. But I warn you, there are alarms throughout this building, and if you're here for anything other than her well-being, I can have the police here in seconds."

"I'm only here for her, Doctor," Colt replied evenly.

The doctor locked the door and without turning toward them, said, "Bring her in here."

They followed him into a nearby examination room. Colt removed the blanket from her shoulders, and Lauren climbed up on to the table.

"You're welcome to wait out there in the hallway," Bridgeton said.

"No," Colt told him flatly. "I stay with her."

The two eyed one another, as if a silent debate were going on between them. The standstill lasted only seconds. Dr. Bridgeton lost. "You can sit over there." He nodded toward a nearby chair.

"Thanks," Colt muttered before he sat down.

Then the doctor's total attention was turned to Lauren. He checked her eyes, her ears. He asked her questions the entire time.

"Are you on any medication?"

"No."

"How are you sleeping?"

"Not very well."

"Has there been any sign of fever?"

"I don't think so."

He put an electronic thermometer in her mouth. Lauren held it under her tongue and waited until the device beeped.

"No fever now," Bridgeton noted, looking at the readout. "As a matter of fact, you're a little cooler than normal. Are you keeping your food down?"

"I don't feel like eating," Lauren replied. "Nothing tastes good. But what I've had has stayed down."

"Is there a chance you could be pregnant?"

Lauren didn't reply for a long moment. It was such a long moment that the doctor halted in his examination of her to search her face.

"Is there?"

Lauren's gaze fell on Colt. Their eyes locked, and another long moment passed.

"Last night..." Lauren said, without taking her eyes from Colt's.

"I see." There was nothing but professionalism in the doctor's tone. "Were you feeling ill before this time?"

Lauren had to think for a moment. "Yes, yes, I think so. Maybe."

"That sounds pretty definite," he muttered. He noticed the bandage on her hand. "What happened here?"

"I—I cut it with a butcher knife," she stammered.

If the doctor doubted her explanation in any way, he didn't show it. He took a pair of scissors and removed the gauze to examine the cut.

"When did you do this?"

"Yesterday afternoon," Lauren replied, biting her lip.

"It probably should have had a few stitches, but it looks to be healing well on its own. I'll give you a few butterfly bandages to keep on it. They should help," he told her, putting a few fresh bandages on her cut now.

"There's no swelling, no outward sign of infection," Dr. Bridgeton said as he felt the glands beneath her chin. He took out a stethoscope and placed the end of it inside her collar to listen to her heart. For several long moments, the room was silent.

"I hear a heart murmur," said Bridgeton. He took the stethoscope from his ears. "Were you aware you have a murmur?"

"No," replied Lauren.

Bridgeton raised a brow. "Well, it could be nothing. Many people have them and never know it. But we should probably plan to do a few tests this week, just to make sure."

"All right," Lauren agreed. "Could that be what's making me sick, Doctor?"

The doctor shrugged slightly. "It's possible that you could be coming down with an infection of the mitral valve, but I think we'd see other signs of infection, such as swollen glands and sore throat and fever. We'll check everything out, just to make sure."

Colt stiffened at his words, at the thought that Lauren might have a heart problem. All this time he'd thought only of protecting her against Dillon Waters. Now that sounded incredibly easy compared to the possibility that she was sick with something that could kill her. No, Colt thought, pushing the thoughts aside. She was going to be fine. Dr. Bridgeton didn't sound all that worried.

"I'll give you some antibiotic just in case, until we find out for sure what's causing it," the doctor went on. He moved on with his examination.

He took Lauren's blood pressure. "It's a little low," he pointed out.

"It usually is," Lauren replied.

He lifted Lauren's shirt and placed his stethoscope on her back. "Take a deep breath."

She complied.

"Another. And another."

The look on his face was the same as when he'd discovered her heart murmur, Colt noticed. Colt leaned forward in his chair. "What is it, Doc?" he asked, trying to keep his sudden alarm out of his voice.

"You're wheezing, Miss Baker," the doctor replied. "Do you suffer from asthma?"

"No."

"Then it's probably a touch of bronchitis. I'll take some blood to send off to the lab for a few tests. If it is bronchitis, the antibiotics should take care of it."

It took a few minutes for the doctor to take two test tubes of Lauren's blood and label the samples.

"Well, that's about all I can do until I get the blood results back and you can get a few tests run. I'll have to send you to the hospital for those. We'll set up some times this week. So call me."

"All right," Lauren promised. "But is there anywhere I could go besides the hospital?"

"No, not here in Rock Hill."

Colt stood up and moved to stand close to her. "I'll go with you, if you want me to," he said softly, remembering her fear of hospitals.

"Thanks," she replied, offering him a small smile.

"Until then, get plenty of rest and drink lots of fluids," Dr. Bridgeton instructed.

"I'll see that she does," Colt put in.

"While we're here, could you take a look at him, too, Doctor?" Lauren asked, indicating Colt.

"Lauren . . ." Colt began.

"What's the matter with him?"

"Nothing," Colt put in.

Lauren spoke at same time. "He was bitten by a dog this morning."

The doctor looked from Colt to Lauren and back to Colt again. "You two lead busy lives, don't you?"

Neither of them offered any reply.

"Sit up here and let me take a look at that bite," he said.

Colt thought of refusing, and the look he threw at Lauren told her he just might do it. But the look she sent back told him he'd better not.

He didn't. After helping her down from the table, he climbed up himself, working the buttons of his shirt. He opened it just far enough for the doctor to see the bite, not wanting to have to remove his gun.

"Is there a rest room I could use?" Lauren asked.

The doctor nodded toward the door. "Out that door and directly to the left."

Lauren looked at Colt. "I'll be right back."

Colt was about to stop her and make her wait until he could check it out, but just then Dr. Bridgeton touched the bite mark on his arm. The pain it caused took his attention just long enough for Lauren to slip out the door.

Fine, he thought. He gave her the same option as he had when she went upstairs to put on her jeans, even though this time she didn't know it. She had her three minutes before he went after her.

"Has this dog been quarantined?" the doctor asked, taking Colt's attention again.

"No."

"He should be. Has his owner been notified?"

"Lauren was—is—his owner."

Bridgeton stopped in his examination of the bite to look at Colt. "It was Miss Baker's dog?" He stepped away slightly.

"Yes."

The doctor took his stethoscope from his neck and absently slipped it into his pocket, his eyes never leaving Colt. "You said before that her life was in danger. Is it possible that you are the danger?" he asked slowly.

Colt held his gaze. "She came to me and told me that she felt someone wanted to kill her," he explained, his own words coming out just as slowly, just as precisely. "After some investigation, I found what she said to be true."

"So why did her dog attack you?"

"I don't know," Colt lied.

"Has he ever bitten anyone else?"

"I don't know," he lied again.

"Do you know if the dog's had his shots?"

"Lauren said he has."

"The police should be notified. This should be reported."

Colt let out a breath. It was enough that he had to watch his back, as well as Lauren's, because of Dillon Waters. Now he was being forced to justify himself to a doctor.

"The police have been notified, and they've done all they can," he said. Short of arresting Lauren, he thought. And, as he thought of Lauren, he realized her three minutes were up.

"I'll give you an antibiotic, as well. And you can call me in a week and let me know how this is healing."

"Good," said Colt. He pulled his shirt over his shoulder as he slid down from the table. "I've got to go find her now."

His heart shuddered then, at the sound that came from beyond the door where Lauren had gone minutes before. *Lauren!*

Her sharp "No!" reached him, and he knew that whatever was happening to her, no matter how fast he reached that door, he was already too late.

CHAPTER FIFTEEN

Lauren had found the rest room without any problem. And after she finished, she'd stood at the sink and looked at her worn reflection in the mirror for a long moment. She remembered the look Colt had given her when she mentioned the bite on his shoulder, but that was just too bad. She hadn't wanted to come to the doctor's office, either, but he'd forced her. He deserved to have his own turn at being poked and prodded.

She took a deep breath and tried to force the nausea from her stomach, but it refused to leave, remaining right in the pit of her insides, like some ever-burning fire that she couldn't put out.

She was so incredibly tired. If she had lain back on the examining table, she probably would have gone right to sleep. Maybe this was just some kind of flu, she thought. But if it was, it was surely the worst case she'd ever had.

She glanced briefly at the specimen cups lined up on a shelf near the mirror, and thought for a moment about the doctor's questions regarding her possible pregnancy. Chances were, she wasn't pregnant. And even if she was, she couldn't be certain for a few weeks. But that didn't stop her from wondering about it. What would her and Colt's child look like? Would it be a little girl with her red hair and Colt's dark eyes or a boy who looked just like his father, with dark hair and dark skin? She could just imagine Colt's twinkling eyes as he looked at his child. Even more, she could imagine the love that would surge through her at seeing him with their child.

Was she wrong to wish for such a future? No, she answered her own question. Right now, she would have given almost anything to have that kind of life with Colt. To share a child with him. She had the right to wish for a future, and with Dillon Waters out there wanting her dead, she'd be willing to take almost any kind of future.

She bent over the sink and splashed cool water on her face, careful not to wet the bandage on her hand. The water was cool enough to cause her to shiver.

She dried her face with a paper towel, tossed it in a nearby can and opened the door.

And found herself face-to-face with Dillon Waters.

The sudden impact of seeing him caused her to stumble backward until she collided with the sink. She forced herself to look away from him before he could put her under his spell.

The fear that washed over her was strong enough to take her breath away. He stood there, unmoving. She could feel his presence, could feel the coldness of him, and she shivered again.

You can look at me, Lauren, he said softly, his voice sounding raspy.

She shook her head and refused to answer.

I'm not going to hurt you, he persisted.

"You said that before," she whispered, her throat so tight with terror that she could hardly force the words out. "I don't believe you."

No matter what Norbrook told you, I've never lied to you.

"But you've already hurt me," she pointed out.

It wasn't something I wanted to do, but you made it necessary.

He was silent then, and Lauren thought perhaps he had left. Yet she could still feel him there, and she had to fight the urge to look at him.

I won't hurt you now, Lauren. Please look at me.

"How can I believe you?"

I promised to kill Norbrook first, and because I still have time, I'll do my best to live up to that promise.

The thought of him even hurting Colt was enough to send her heart slamming against the wall of her chest. She couldn't help but look at him now.

She blinked against the horror of the way Dillon looked. His face was the color of oatmeal, looking more like chalk than her own.

Yes, love, he said in answer to her unasked question. *You and I are both sick. And the only way for us to get well is to get rid of Norbrook and be together.*

"Never," she whispered.

He smiled, and she saw that one of his front teeth was missing. Lauren stared at it. Dear God, was that what came next for her? Were her teeth going to fall out? A moan escaped her at the thought.

"That's why you're doing this, isn't it? You're using me to hurt Colt, aren't you?"

I started out only wanting you. But if it gives Norbrook the pain he deserves, then it's just an added bonus.

"You used Mav to try to kill him, didn't you?" she spit out.

I have such a way with animals, he replied, still smiling. *I was so disappointed when it turned out to be unsuccessful.* He took a step closer.

There was nowhere for Lauren to go. She was already pressed up against the sink. His coldness penetrated the air. She couldn't think, she could hardly breathe. "Why did you use the dog?" she asked. "If you want Colt dead so bad, why not just shoot him or cut his throat like you would have mine?"

That would be too easy. I so enjoy the challenge. Besides, Norbrook deserves to go by different means—something slower, with a lot more pain, don't you think? And I see another chance coming. I just hope it will come before you and I are out of time. Time is so precious, don't you agree? His smile grew.

"You used the sledgehammer from my stable, too, didn't you?" she asked.

It was handy, he replied. *It's too bad Norbrook wasn't around for that.*

"Where is it?" she asked.

I knew the police probably wouldn't be able to connect it to you, and they wouldn't arrest you and take you from the safe clutches of Norbrook. So I simply put it back where I got it.

"How nice of you," she snapped.

You'll find I can be very nice to you in many ways, Lauren.

He reached up slowly and placed his fingertips on her cheek. His touch was like ice, and she shivered. "Don't touch me!"

Try and stop me.

She tried. She tried to turn her head away, but he brought his other hand up and cupped her face, keeping her from moving. She could feel the cold strength of his fingers, and another shiver of fear moved through her.

"Why are you doing this to me?" she cried.

Because I love you. It's as simple as that.

"But why?" she asked.

He chuckled at her question. *Why? You need to ask? All you need to do is look in the mirror to see why. I loved you from the moment I saw you.*

"But how? How can you love me so much? I don't even know you. I never saw you until the day you tried to rob the Rock Hill Bank."

He smiled lovingly and slowly shook his head. *You just don't remember me. And that's why I'm here now. It's time for you to remember, Lauren. It's time for you to remember what we had together, what almost was. Only then will you be able to see that Norbrook is just in the way. And then you'll be able to let him go and give us the chance that we deserve. You will live up to the promise of love you gave me.*

She refused to believe him, and wished she could refuse to listen to him just as easily. "No, I would never have made any promise of love to you. You're nothing but a lying murderer."

That was before you, Lauren. You know things aren't the same. That was a different life. You gave me a reason to change.

"You're not any different. You haven't changed a bit. You still tried to kill Colt, you killed the caretaker at the cemetery, and what you did to my dog was unspeakable."

But necessary.

"Leave me alone," she pleaded. She could only whisper through her tight throat, no matter how much she wished she could scream and get Colt's attention.

Never. Never, my love, he replied calmly. *Not until you are mine. You promised.*

She tried to shake her head in denial, but his hands held her still. "I never promised," she said. Or had she? The memory touched her now, just as it had the first time she looked at him, through her kitchen window, and she shuddered at the thought that there might be more she couldn't remember.

Think of my touch, he said, his fingers caressing her.

"It's cold," she said, still trying to scream, still trying to pull away. She blinked away the tears of fear that came to her eyes. She absolutely refused to let him see her lose control.

Think of the date, Lauren, he went on.

"What date?" His words made no sense. Lauren felt more confused than ever.

October the seventeenth, the date of my death. Think of my kiss, and my holding you in my arms, and you will remember. Think of that day in October. Think of where you were.

"Oh, God…" He was going to kiss her. His icy, dead lips were already drawing closer, and this time Lauren knew she wasn't dreaming. This was real. She was going to be sick. She was going to faint. "Colt!" she cried. It came out sounding more like a groan.

Then his words hit her, and she remembered the date's significance. The memory of the promise she'd made to him suddenly came flooding through her mind.

Yes, I'll stay here with you forever. We'll be together forever.

She felt as if she were choking on the memory. She could remember hearing herself say it just before she was taken away from him. She wished the words had never left her mouth, but she had indeed said them. She'd said them to Dillon Waters.

She'd been so afraid, and he'd been there with her. His arms around her had been a comfort in a frightening place. But it was over, and it was never to be again. She understood that. Why couldn't he? And a more horrifying truth came to her. She understood, too, what would have to happen if she was to live up to her promise. The only problem was, *live* was the wrong word.

"No!" She'd finally gotten out more than a whisper. But that one word was all her voice had the strength for. Yet her mind cried out again and again. No! No! She couldn't have made that promise to Dillon Waters. It couldn't be true. She couldn't have been in his arms, looking up into his eyes, believing the two of them should stay together.

Fortunately, his lips never reached hers. The reality of her situation became too much for her senses to handle. Before his touch could reach her, she slipped away from him, sliding down to the floor. Falling in a faint to the safety of darkness.

She woke to the muffled sound of voices and the feel of hands touching her.

She fought against the hands, knowing they were Dillon Waters's hands. "No! No, let me go!"

"Lauren."

"Let me go!"

"Lauren, it's me. Look at me." He was grasping her shoulders so tightly that it hurt.

She forced her eyes open and looked up, meeting Colt's gaze.

"What happened?"

"He was here. He was in here."

"Who?" Dr. Bridgeton asked.

Both Lauren and Colt ignored his question.

She didn't need to tell Colt any more. He looked at Dr. Bridgeton. "Stay with her. Don't leave her for anything." Pulling out his gun, he turned toward the hall.

Lauren caught his arm. "Be careful. He really plans to kill you."

He nodded, and there was such tenderness in his eyes that it was all she could do to let him go. He turned and moved cautiously down the hall, going off to search for Dillon Waters. Lauren and the doctor watched him until he moved out of sight.

Seconds became minutes. The building was silent, so silent it threatened to drive Lauren mad. She waited for any sound from Colt. And she silently prayed that he'd be all right. All this time, she had thought that being afraid for her own life was the most horrifying feeling possible. Now she found that it was nothing compared to the fear she had for Colt.

"Someone really wants to hurt you," Dr. Bridgeton said. It was a statement, not a question, indicating that he now believed their story.

"He means to hurt us both," she responded softly, still praying for Colt's safety.

"Let me help you back into the examination room. You can lie down on the table," said Dr. Bridgeton, taking her arm. "Then perhaps you can tell me all about your situation."

Lauren looked at him skeptically, and pulled away from his touch.

He returned her look, but his was filled with confusion.

"I'll wait here for Colt," she stated firmly. From her position, she had a clear view of the hallway. She could run down it much quicker from here if she had to, either to reach Colt or to reach the door. Besides, she had no intention of telling the doctor anything specific about Dillon Waters. With her illness, the cut on her hand and the bite on Colt's shoulder, it was hard to figure what the good doctor already thought of them. If she told him that the man who wanted to kill her and Colt was already dead, he'd probably have them both shipped off to some asylum.

No way. She wasn't going to let something like that happen, not while she and Colt still had some hope of getting through this and sharing a life together.

"All right," the doctor agreed. "But if you intend to wait here, at least lean back and try to relax. You fainted, and it may take a few minutes for your body to recover."

Lauren tried to relax, but it wasn't easy, with the waiting and the silence.

A few minutes later, Colt returned, as silently as he'd gone. She breathed a sigh of relief. "He's gone," he told them.

"Who?" Dr. Bridgeton asked again.

And once more Lauren and Colt ignored his question.

"How did he get in here?" Lauren asked.

"A window in one of the examining rooms is open."

"Who?" the doctor persisted.

Colt turned his attention to Dr. Bridgeton for the first time. "It's better for you if you don't know." As soon as the words were out, Colt wondered if that was true. Dillon had killed the caretaker at the cemetery, and it wouldn't be hard for him to do the same to the doctor. "On the other hand, Doctor," he said, "it's probably best if you go right home and lock yourself in your house."

"Tell me what's going on," the doctor pleaded. "Who was in here?"

"We can't tell," Lauren replied. "You'd think we were crazy if we told you."

"She's right," added Colt. "All we can tell you is that someone is trying to kill her—"

"No," she said, interrupting. "He plans to kill us both. And now that you've helped us, he may try to hurt you, too."

"But—" the doctor began.

"But nothing," said Colt. "Come on, Lauren. We've got to get out of here. We're not safe here."

The doctor seemed to sense this was a losing battle. "At least let me get you the antibiotics and butterfly bandages I promised. And you—" he looked at Colt "—should have a tetanus shot."

They stayed only long enough to get the medication and bandages. Then, Colt wrapped Lauren in the cotton blanket again and helped her back to the truck.

Except for the waiting rifle, the truck was empty, and Colt helped her climb in. Once they were inside, Colt started the engine, and the two of them sat quietly for a long moment. The only sound around them was the heavily falling rain and the swishing of the truck wipers.

"What are you waiting for?" Lauren asked.

"I want to watch Dr. Bridgeton leave, so I know he's all right."

Colt put his arm around her and pulled her close to his side, and the two of them waited.

Within a few minutes, they saw Dr. Bridgeton's silhouetted form exit the building. He turned and locked the door behind him before hurrying to his car. Colt waited until he heard the doctor's car start before he put the truck in gear and left the parking lot.

The night was unusually dark. The clouds covered whatever moon there was, and the rain fell down in sheets. Thunder rumbled now and again, but there was no lightning making its way through the darkness.

Colt was anxious, gripping the steering wheel with one hand until his knuckles were white. He held on to Lauren just as tightly until she said, "Colt, you're hurting me."

"I'm sorry." He let her go quickly, as though his fingers were burned. "I just wouldn't be surprised if Dillon Waters came jumping out in front of the truck or something."

"I know the feeling," she muttered. "I thought my heart would stop when I opened that bathroom door to find him standing there waiting for me."

"What exactly did he say to you?"

Lauren told him. With her body feeling exhausted and sick, with the terror still swirling through her, her words poured out slowly. Yet she told him precisely, word for word.

"And he's sick, too," she concluded. "Only sicker. His face looks more like paste. And he's missing a tooth." She put one hand over her own mouth, as though she were hoping the action would hold off what would inevitably happen to her. "Oh . . ." she moaned. "After all those years of braces, I don't want to lose my teeth."

"You won't," he promised her. "We're going to get through this. You'll see."

She shook her head, and her cheek brushed against his upper arm. "No, we won't."

He chuckled, forcing himself to sound light and confident. "What? You've lost faith in me after all this, have you?"

It was a long moment before she could reply. "No, it has nothing to do with my faith in you."

"Then what?" He glanced over at her to see tears coursing down her cheeks.

Her words were tight, racked by sobs she couldn't hold back. "I made him a promise." She paused and pressed her face against his shoulder, her crying muffled against him.

Colt waited.

"I remember," she said finally, her voice filled with her tears. "I—I remember everything. I remember being so afraid, and Dillon holding me in his arms, asking me to stay with him. I remember saying I would stay with him forever."

"When did you promise this?" Colt asked. His arm tightened around her, and she tried to snuggle more comfortably against him.

"It—it was that day when I had my car accident, during those few minutes when I was dead. I remember thinking about it days later, after I was awake and thinking clearly." She had to pause to catch her breath, and still she wasn't able to bring her sobbing under control. Her words, when she continued, were broken. "It was...nothing more than a dream. At least...I thought it was a dream."

They reached the inn, and Colt pulled into the driveway and turned off the truck. He moved to face her squarely. "What exactly are you saying, Red?"

"I'm saying I had my car accident the same day you shot *him*," she explained.

"Are you trying to tell me you met Dillon Waters on the other side of life, and promised to stay with him forever?" Colt asked, clearly not believing a word.

"I don't know," she admitted. She sniffed. "When I think about it, it still seems like nothing more than a dream I had." And yet the cold horror of it was clamped around her like a vise. She wiped her eyes absently. "He held me and told me not to be afraid," she said, her words still broken. She clenched her teeth to keep them from chattering. "He asked me if I'd stay with him forever, and I said I would. The next thing I remember is waking up in a hospital bed."

He chuckled again. "That's the craziest damn thing I've ever heard. Let's go in. I think I need a drink." He reached back to unlock his door.

"Why?" she asked, stopping him, her voice rising in frustration and fear. "Why can't you believe me? What time did you shoot Dillon, or don't you remember?"

He sighed loudly, forcing himself to be patient. "Of course I remember. I wrote it on at least five hundred reports. It was 2:37 in the afternoon. Not 2:38 or 2:36, but 2:37, right on the dot. Hell . . ." He paused to sigh heavily again. "I thought I'd be doing the paperwork on that for the rest of my life."

He glanced over at Lauren, and saw the shock and horror in her expression. "What?" he asked. "What's the matter?"

"Oh, my God..." she moaned. She covered her face with her hands, as though she couldn't bear to look out into the night. "Oh, my God . . ."

"What? Lauren?"

"How can you be so damned calm about this?" she yelled at him, taking her hands from her face. "Don't you see? That was the time the police reported that my car accident occurred.'' She was nearly screaming at him. ''That's what you consider a coincidence, huh?''

''Yes, Lauren,'' he said, trying to pull her close again. ''But, Red, that's all it is—a coincidence.''

''I don't believe that, and neither do you!'' she said in a frightened voice. She wanted to shake him, hard, until he understood the reality of what she was saying.

He offered her a smile. ''Well, then, perhaps it's time to start wearing garlic to frighten away the vampires, and stock up on our silver bullets to shoot the werewolves with.'' To Lauren's horror, there was laughter in his voice.

God, he really didn't believe her. And she couldn't decide which was worse—her being able to finally see the truth or Colt's refusing to see it. Finally her serious expression softened. ''No,'' she told him, her voice still high-pitched. ''I can't believe it was just a coincidence. What do I have to do to convince you?''

''Let's take this inside, Red,'' he said, still sounding amused. ''Where it's warm and dry.''

He leaned forward to kiss her, and Lauren leaned up to meet his lips. His kiss was soft, gentle, so much like their first kiss in his cabin.

Releasing her mouth slowly, he reached back to open the door, pulling on the handle just enough to release the latch. Suddenly the door on his side was jerked open, and he was wrenched away from her, out of the truck and into the rain.

Dillon Waters stood there over him. And when Colt tried to gain his equilibrium, Waters struck him in the jaw, just as he had before. Even if Colt hadn't been off-balance, the punch would probably have been enough to knock Colt off his feet. He landed flat on his back in the rain-slicked mud of the driveway.

Dillon looked into the truck and smiled at Lauren. "I love doing that," he said with a laugh. "I love hitting him so much I'd like to beat him to death slowly. But, alas, my love, I'm afraid there isn't enough time."

He reached into the truck beside her legs and grabbed the rifle.

He almost had it out of the truck by the time Lauren realized his intention.

"No!" She grabbed the butt of the rifle and tried to pull it back into the truck.

His eyes met hers through the darkness. He was completely soaked, his light hair plastered to his head. He was so pale, he seemed to glow in the darkness, appearing almost translucent. "I'm sorry, my love. You knew from the beginning this was how it would be. Now let go. Time is getting away from us." The gentleness of his voice shook her with terror.

"No. I won't let you."

"You must."

"No." She looked right into his eyes, to show him she could be as strong as he was.

"Let go, Lauren."

When she refused, he pulled on his end of the rifle with all his strength. But Lauren maintained her grip, and Dillon's jerk was strong enough to pull her right out of the truck, along with the rifle.

The rain beat down, drenching her instantly. She had a hard time seeing through it, and she could barely maintain her balance in the mud beneath her feet. The wind was blowing so hard that for a mere instant she thought that if she didn't let go of the rifle to grab the door of the truck, she might just be swept away with it.

And then Lauren stopped struggling suddenly and looked around. Her eyes met Dillon's, and they both realized something was different.

Colt was gone.

CHAPTER SIXTEEN

"**W**here is he?" Dillon asked, grinding the question out through a clenched jaw.

"I don't know any more than you do," she replied, her voice filled with all the hostility she could muster.

He grabbed her suddenly. His grip on her arm felt tighter than a vise, threatening to cut off her circulation. She tried to pull away and found it impossible. All that happened was that her feet slid on the wet ground.

"Norbrook!" Dillon called, yelling into the wind. He stepped away from the truck, taking Lauren with him, and looked around through the darkness and rain. In his other hand, he held the rifle.

Lauren couldn't see anything more than dark outlines of familiar objects. Something that resembled the lid of one of Lauren's trash cans blew past them, looking like nothing more than a large flying disc. If they had gone a few steps more, it would have hit them. Too bad it hadn't hit Dillon, she thought.

"Norbrook!" Dillon called again. "If you come out now, she still has a chance!"

Lauren didn't know where Colt was, but she doubted he would hear the threat unless he was standing right in front of them. Dillon's voice was swept away by the strong wind the moment his words left his mouth.

She also knew Dillon was lying. She had no chance, none at all. He wanted to kill her, and he meant to succeed.

They took a few more steps forward, and a sudden gust almost swept Lauren's feet out from under her again. She would have fallen if Dillon hadn't pulled her closer to him.

"This is your last chance, Norbrook!" Dillon called out. After a moment, he said to Lauren, "Which do you prefer, my love? Shall I shoot you or strangle you? I'll let you decide. I'm only sorry that I can't live up to my promise of killing Norbrook first, but I don't have the time to wait."

Dear God, she thought, the time had come. Terror swept through her, leaving her completely numb. There was no way in the world she could answer such a question. She could hardly breathe. She expected her life to flash before her eyes at any moment.

Thoughts did come to her, flashing through her mind. But they were thoughts of Colt, and she wished she could tell him that she knew he'd done his best to save her. She should have known that it was impossible. She thought of the way he'd made love to her, and wished that kind of happiness had found her earlier in life. She wished only for enough time to tell him how much she loved him.

She did love Colt. Nothing else mattered, once that realization came to her. It gave her new strength. It gave her new purpose.

"Don't think of him," Dillon said, reading her thoughts.

"No," she said, refusing to agree to his demand. She remembered her words to Colt about never giving up, and she vowed not to do so now. Not when she had found love. Not now that she had found the most important reason for never giving up.

"What?" Dillon asked, as though he were surprised that she was still defying him after all this. He looked at her, his light blue eyes glowing eerily in the dark.

She was about to lash out at him when something came toward them through the rain. She couldn't make out exactly what it was until it drew closer.

Then a sound touched her through the sweeping wind and the beating rain. It was the whinny of a horse.

Suddenly, she could see it clearly, and her heart slammed against her chest at the sight of what was approaching her.

It was Colt. And he was riding Lightning, the black horse from the stable.

He looked just as she had once pictured him—a tall brave atop a majestic horse. The only thing missing was the feathered headdress, she thought.

Then another thought came to her, and this one was laced with fear. Lightning, in all his nearsightedness, was likely to run right past them and crash into the side of her truck. That would be the end of any chance either of them might have.

To her surprise, Lightning didn't crash. At Colt's command, the horse swept past them, Colt attempting to reach down and sweep her away from Dillon as they flew past. He nearly succeeded. Lauren felt the brush of his hand across her stomach. But Dillon managed to pull her away just before Colt could grab her.

Lauren jerked against Dillon, trying to escape his grip. She kicked out at him. "Let me go!" When he didn't, she tried to reach him with her free hand and scratch his face.

He only laughed in the wind. It was a haunting, empty sound that froze her heart. "Don't you know by now that you can't hurt me, my love?" Then he turned his attention back to the other man.

Colt had turned Lightning around and was about to charge toward them again. Dillon raised the rifle, and Lauren felt the barrel of it pressing against her neck.

At Dillon's action, everything stopped.

Colt brought Lightning to a halt just yards away.

In the same instant, Lauren thought her heart would fail. She thought of the bank robbery, and the heart-stopping fear that had consumed her when Dillon first pointed his gun at her. She remembered the pain and the terror when he'd shot her in the arm, and she couldn't stop the shiver that passed through her. Oh, God, she didn't want to die this way!

At Colt's command, Lightning slowly walked closer, halting right in front of them.

"Let her go," Colt yelled down to them.

"Never," Dillon replied. His voice was still loud, but it had taken on a gentle, caressing tone that was enough to send Lauren's stomach into spasms. Just to prove his point, Dillon leaned over and placed a cold, wet kiss on her temple.

Lauren trembled at the contact, and was certain she was going to be sick at any moment.

Dillon took the barrel of the rifle away from her and pointed it at Colt. "I guess it looks as though I'll get to keep my promise after all."

"No!" Lauren screamed out. "Don't hurt him! If you want me, then take me! But don't hurt him! I love him!"

"No!" It was Colt's turn to yell out.

"You don't love him, Lauren," Dillon put in, ignoring Colt. "You've had a good time with him the last few days, but that's all it is. That's all it ever will be. It could never be anything more." His voice flowed through her like ice-cold water.

Colt swung his leg over the horse's head and slid to the ground.

"Let her go," he said again. "Can't you see she doesn't love you? Can't you see she doesn't even want you?"

Dillon laughed again—another frightening, hollow sound that seemed to reach into Lauren and touch her very soul with coldness. "It doesn't matter," he said. "She did once, and she will again."

"Never!" said Lauren. "I know what you are now. I didn't then."

"But you promised!" Dillon yelled.

Getting through this alive no longer seemed as important as getting through Dillon's stubbornness to make him understand that she would *never* love him.

"Did she?" Colt put in, stepping closer.

Oh, please don't come any closer, Lauren silently begged.

Colt couldn't hear her unspoken plea, but ignored the imploring look in her eyes. He came even closer. "Did she promise?" he asked.

Dillon didn't reply.

"Did she say 'I promise'? Or did you just ask her to stay, and she said yes?" He paused to stare at Dillon.

Lauren could feel Dillon's confusion. She could feel it sweeping through him everywhere his body touched hers. He still refused to answer.

She decided to speak for herself. "No, I didn't say 'I promise.' I never said that at all. I felt alone and frightened, and Dillon was there. That's all. Maybe I felt grateful, but I don't remember feeling anything else.''

"No! That's a lie!" shouted Dillon. In his growing anger, he shifted his hold on Lauren, attempting to turn her and force her to look at him.

That quickly, Colt reached out and grabbed her, pulling her out of Dillon's grasp. Dillon reached for her again, but his fingers merely caught the wet fabric of her shirt, ripping her sleeve.

Then she was in Colt's arms, and together they faced Dillon Waters. Standing against him, his one arm around her, Lauren felt that the two of them could face down anything. But her fear grew as Dillon raised the rifle again. "I don't love you! Can't you understand that?" she screamed at him.

"Go ahead," said Colt. His voice was quite calm. "Shoot us. Just make sure you shoot both of us, so that we can be together even in death.''

Lauren shivered at his words.

And Dillon hesitated.

"Think about it, Waters," Colt went on, stalling for time. "Think about it hard. If you shoot us, we'll be together forever, and I promise you—and, yes, it's a promise I intend to keep—that between Lauren and me, there will never be room for you. I will love her forever. Never shall we part—not even in death.''

To add to Lauren's horror, Colt let go of her just enough that he could step slightly in front of her. "So go ahead," he said again. "Shoot me first. But before you shoot Lauren, take a close look at her. She's not looking so pale, is she?''

Dillon did look, and said nothing. He continued to aim the rifle at them.

"Why? Don't you wonder? It's because she's losing her doubts about my love. That was why your sickness was able to touch her in the first place, because she doubted my feelings. That was your hold on her, but you no longer have it." Colt turned back again to look at her. "Look at me, Lauren."

She did.

"That was why you weren't sick when I made love to you. Because it was impossible for you to doubt what you were feeling. So let go of your doubt now. Let go of all of it. Know that what I feel for you is true." Colt reached out to place his palm gently on her cheek.

Despite the cold rain on her face, his touch warmed her instantly.

"Lauren," Dillon cut in, "it's not in his destiny to love you."

He was trying to confuse her. Lauren knew that. And he was doing a good job of it, despite her efforts not to believe him. She remembered Colt's words—*Destiny be damned.*

Colt never took his eyes from hers. "My grandfather spoke of my destiny before I left the reservation. He said that if I left, I would know only grief. And he said that after the grief there would be fire. I never knew what he meant.

"Well, Red, now I know." He looked deep into her eyes, seeing into her soul. "I know he was right. I did have grief after I couldn't save that teller at the bank. And afterward, there was fire. But you were the fire. It was the fire of your hair. He meant the fire of your love, and the fire of your passion. My grandfather was talking about you. I saw it last night. I felt it when I kissed you."

A tear slid down Lauren's cheek.

"And you gave me so much more, more than I ever could have expected. You brought me love. I love you, Lauren. I think I must have loved you from that first time I saw you, before I knew you. Then, when you brought me those newspaper articles and I saw Dillon Waters again, I was terrified that I couldn't stop him from hurting you, just as I couldn't stop him from killing before." Colt's voice was harsh, bursting with emotion, filled with his love for her.

"Oh, Colt . . ." she whispered.

"And when I kissed you," he went on, "last night in my cabin, I felt the passion in you. I felt the fire, and I knew it was filled with everything that's right. I knew it would see us through this." He smiled down at her. "And that getting through this would mean a whole new chance at life."

They might have been all alone in the world, the way he was looking at her, touching her. They might have been in a place where there was only room for the two of them.

Then, in a single instant, one split second of time, Dillon Waters destroyed the place they had found. He pulled the trigger of the rifle.

Lauren thought what she heard was a loud, sharp crack of thunder. But then something hard slammed into her, with enough force to knock her away from Colt. There was instant pain in her shoulder, running down her arm and throughout the rest of her body. The rain hit her face, and she sensed that she was now lying on the ground, although she couldn't seem to remember just how she'd come to be there. She heard a pounding sound, and it took a moment for her to realize it was Lightning running past her. She forced her eyes open and looked up at Colt, who was leaning over her, yelling at her. But his words made little sense. He was telling her to hold on. But hold on to what? The fire in her body was unbearably painful. Much to her relief, blessed darkness overtook her, washing it all away....

The cry that tore from Colt touched the wind. "Lauren! Lauren!" No. He wouldn't let her die. He wouldn't let her leave him. He tore off his shirt and stuffed it beneath hers, pressing it against the gunshot wound between her shoulder and her collarbone. He pressed it firmly, trying to stop the flow of blood.

Behind him, Dillon Waters reminded him of his presence with another hollow laugh. "You can't help her," he said in a teasing voice.

Colt turned slowly to face his enemy. The smile on Dillon's face turned his fear and rage into cold, heartless fury. He lunged, the sudden movement taking Dillon completely off guard. He collided with him, knocking the rifle out of his hands, and the two of them went tumbling down in the mud and wet grass.

Colt managed to get on top and pin Dillon to the ground, thinking he had Dillon where he could finally finish him. He had his hands on Dillon's throat, squeezing. "You bastard!" he growled.

But he underestimated Dillon's great strength and was unprepared for the fist that hit him in the midsection. It doubled him over instantly, and Dillon was able to shove him off.

Dillon looked down at him, and smiled his ghostly smile. "You convinced me, Norbrook. I won't take a chance and kill you, but I will give you a bit of pain, so you won't forget me anytime soon." He kick Colt's thigh, and was about to kick him a second time when something hit him. Something hard.

It was the wind. It was suddenly blowing strong enough to push Dillon away. Colt was forced to roll with it twice before he could dig his hands into the ground and anchor himself.

It swirled around them with the growing strength of a cyclone. It shook Lauren's truck and sent debris flying past them. The swing on her front porch beat madly against the house.

Colt watched in shock and wonder. The rain blew in a swirl with the leaves, until it was strong enough to lift Dillon right from the ground.

Waters reached out, grasping for anything to hold on to, and met only the wind. "No!" he cried out. "Not without you, Lauren!" He reached for her and managed to grasp the sleeve of her shirt.

Colt realized what was happening. Dillon's time was up. And though Lauren wasn't dead—at least not yet—Dillon meant to take her with him.

She was caught in Dillon's grip, while the wind began to carry him farther away. To Colt's horror, she was being lifted with Waters, sliding away on the wet grass. After all she'd been through, Dillon was still going to take her back.

No! He couldn't let her keep sliding! With all his strength, Colt reached out with one hand, fighting the wind, and grasped her, catching her other hand. He tried to pull her toward him, fighting the raging wind and the strength of Dillon Waters. He held tight, while Dillon pulled Lauren in the opposite direction. Through the sound of the wind, Colt heard her moan.

The sound filled him with hope. She was alive. Dillon didn't have her yet. Colt still had a chance.

There was a long moment when Lauren was the object of a tug-of-war. Dillon pulled on her shirt, but Colt held fast to her hand, not letting her slide even an inch farther away from him.

"Let her go," Dillon ground out.

"Never," Colt replied, realizing that he had never contemplated the true meaning of that one word until this moment. He heard Lauren groan in pain once more. And although it hurt him deeply to know how she must be hurting, he still welcomed the sound of life from her.

Finally the wind grew too strong, and the fabric of her sleeve, already partially torn from when Dillon had tried to grab her before, ripped away. She fell out of Dillon's grasp and landed near Colt.

The wind blew harder for several more long seconds. Colt fought against it, and held on to Lauren with every ounce of strength he possessed. Pressing himself as flat to the ground as possible, he held her as the wind swirled around them and the rain continued to soak them. From somewhere within the house beyond them, Colt heard glass breaking and assumed the windows could no longer take the pressure of the roaring wind.

And suddenly, Dillon Waters was swept away into the swirl of blowing leaves and debris, disappearing into the night. His mouth opened in a silent scream.

The wind was gradually dying down, leaving only the rain to batter them.

Colt's hold on Lauren lessened, and he pulled himself up to look closer at her. Please don't let her be dead. Not now, he prayed.

"Colt?" she said softly, as though in answer to his prayer.

"I'm right here, Red. Everything's going to be just fine. I'm going to get you to the hospital." He groaned as he tried to stand. After fighting Dillon and fighting to keep from being swept away with the wind, every muscle in his body screamed for rest. But he knew he couldn't wait to replenish his strength. Lauren could die waiting.

He heaved himself to his feet, trying to ignore the pain in his shoulders. He drew her up against him, into his arms, and was forced to pause again for a moment before he could fully stand. She felt so cold and lifeless in his arms. The short distance to her truck seemed like miles to his legs, and he was breathing heavily when he finally managed to slide her into the passenger seat.

He slid behind the wheel and glanced at Lauren's quiet, still form. He could see her chest moving as she breathed. She was still alive. "I'm going to get you to the hospital, and you're going to be fine," he said again. "I'm not going to let you down," he muttered into the silence of the truck before starting it. He paused to cover her with the cotton blanket that was still on the seat. Then he started the wipers and pulled away as fast as the mud-slick drive would allow. Though the wind had died down, the rain continued to fall in heavy sheets, making the drive to the hospital much longer that it should have been.

By the time Colt pulled to a stop in front of the emergency room, he was fighting to remain in control of his own emotions. He had thought Dillon Waters had shown him fear. But that was nothing compared to the fear he was feeling for Lauren right now. She didn't respond to his voice, and she didn't react when he reached over and touched her. Though he could hear her raspy breathing, he was terrified by the amount of blood on her shirt. Could she lose so much blood and still pull through?

He fought to keep himself moving. Grabbing her up in his arms, he carried her to the emergency room entrance.

The hospital was a whirlwind of activity. The doctor in charge, upon seeing Lauren, began issuing orders all around. He threw Colt only a quick glance. "What happened?"

"Gunshot" was all he was able to reply before the doctor barked orders at another woman to get Lauren's vital signs. "Call the surgeon and tell him to get here stat!"

"You'll have to wait out in the waiting room now," a pretty young nurse said, coming close to Colt.

Colt shook his head. "I can't leave her." He thought of her fear of hospitals. After everything they'd been through, after the way he'd saved her life, the way she'd given him a second chance at his own life, he couldn't leave her. What if she died, and Dillon still managed to win? What if she woke to find him nowhere in sight?

"Please?" the nurse begged.

"No, I won't go," Colt replied, staring the nurse in the eye. "You'll have to have me locked up, because even if you drag me out of here, I'll just come back in."

The nurse finally gave in. "All right, but at least stand over here, out of the way."

Colt agreed to that. He watched the team of medical professionals insert tubes and needles into Lauren, trying to "stabilize" her.

A familiar voice grabbed his attention.

"What have we got?" Dr. Bridgeton asked, looking at the patient upon entering the small cubicle.

"I'm glad you could make it so fast, Doctor," the first doctor said.

So Dr. Bridgeton was a surgeon here, Colt realized. Oh, hell....

Dr. Bridgeton slipped on a pair of gloves and took a closer look at Lauren's wound. He hadn't looked at her face yet, and Colt waited for his reaction.

Suddenly, Dr. Bridgeton glanced up and met Colt's gaze. He stopped and stared at Colt for a long moment, and Colt found himself unable to read the look in the doctor's eyes.

Bridgeton took a deep breath. "Don't tell me," he said. "She was cleaning your gun and it accidentally went off, right?" His voice was thick with sarcasm.

Colt stared back and refused to answer.

After a moment, Dr. Bridgeton said, "Get out of my emergency room before I call security."

Colt thought of refusing, but the look in Bridgeton's eyes told him any refusal might bring on more trouble than either he or Lauren needed. He paused a moment before leaving, and drew closer to Lauren, leaning over her.

"Everything I said before, Red, about loving you, all of it was true. Don't ever forget it," he whispered to her still form, not even certain she could hear him. He could only pray that she did. He kissed her cheek softly. He looked up to find Dr. Bridgeton watching him closely.

Even after he had moved outside the small cubicle, he could hear the doctor's voice, loud and clear. "Let's get this woman prepped for surgery, and prepare operating room two. I want everything ready in two minutes."

In the small waiting area a short distance down the hall, Colt gave in to his fatigue and sank into a cushioned chair. Elbows on his knees, he covered his face with his hands. He looked up briefly when they wheeled

Lauren out of the cubicle and down the hall. Then he closed his eyes.

He wasn't even sure how much time passed. Only thoughts of Lauren and prayers for her life passed through his mind.

Footsteps drew his attention, and the stiffness in his neck and shoulders told him he must have dozed off. He was forced to turn his head slowly and blink several times before he could focus on Dr. Bridgeton, who came to stand before him.

And on the two police officers who stood on either side of the doctor.

Colt got to his feet. Still feeling slightly disoriented, he forced himself to stare into the doctor's eyes and ignore the men in uniform beside him. At least it wasn't Benton and McGillin, and Colt was grateful for not having to deal with either of them again.

"Is Lauren going to be all right?" he asked evenly, his brain finally kicking into gear.

"The next twenty-four hours should tell," Bridgeton replied.

Colt glanced at the two policemen.

"I had to report this incident," Bridgeton explained. Then he paused. "I also had to report that because of this and everything that went on during my examination of her in my office earlier, I suspect some type of abuse going on here, Mr. Norbrook."

"We told you before, someone was trying to kill her, and it was that same man who shot her," Colt explained.

"I thought you'd say that, and despite everything that happened, I never saw anyone else in my office, Mr. Norbrook."

"Where is this man now?" one of the officers asked.

Colt didn't reply right away. "I don't know. It was dark, the storm was hitting us full force when we got home. He shot her right after we climbed out of her truck."

He couldn't tell if any of them believed what he said. "Am I under arrest?" he asked.

"Not yet," replied that same officer. "But we'll have to hold you in custody until Miss Baker can tell us what happened."

"Where is she?" he asked. He had to know for sure that she was going to be all right.

"Still in the recovery room," replied Dr. Bridgeton.

The second officer spoke for the first time. "Come with us, please."

Colt wouldn't refuse, now that he knew she was through the worst. But he had the feeling he wasn't going to be here for her when she awoke, and she would have to face her fear of hospitals alone until he could get back to her.

He left with the officers, only to find that the sun was now up. He hadn't just dozed for a few minutes, he had slept through most of the night. The sun was rising in the sky, and he squinted against the sudden brightness of it.

The storm had passed, and Dillon Waters was gone. He had saved Lauren. Colt felt redeemed of all his past guilts. And even though the police were taking him into custody, he felt freer than he had in a long time.

"Do you guys think I could get some dry clothes and a shirt?" he asked the police officers.

"Sure," one replied. "We have a whole bunch of shirts that are stamped City Jail."

Colt laughed. He didn't care what he wore as long as Lauren was all right.

Wake up soon, Red, he thought. I'll be waiting for you.

EPILOGUE

"What? No flowers today? What happened? Did the nurses yell at you and tell you there was no more room here for any more?" Lauren asked, her green eyes sparkling, her voice filled with laughter. She was sitting on the edge of her hospital bed, waiting for him.

Colt smiled, happy to see her looking so healthy. After his last examination, Dr. Bridgeton had been almost puzzled by Lauren's speedy, complete recovery.

"I thought about it," Colt replied, "but I figured since I'm taking you home today, it would be one more bunch that we'd have to carry out of here. I thought I'd bring you some clothes to wear home instead." He set a small bag on the rolling tray table.

"Gee—" she pretended to be disappointed "—and here I thought I was going to get to wear this lovely hospital gown home."

"Oh, no," he said, his voice growing husky. "I brought something I think you'll like much better."

Lauren reached into the bag and pulled out a pair of jeans and Colt's soft cotton shirt. He had washed it for her, and it felt soft to the touch.

Lauren fingered the shirt gently and bit her lip, not looking at him. During her recovery, they had never even brought up the subject of their relationship, and she still didn't quite know where she stood with him.

"You know," she said slowly, "I don't think I ever told you how sorry I was that the police held you in custody."

He smiled again, despite the fact that she wasn't looking at him, wasn't seeing it. "It didn't matter. All that mattered was that you were going to be all right. If I had lost you, I don't think I could have gone on with any kind of a life," he replied. "I'm just sorry I couldn't be here with you when you woke up."

"When you weren't, I knew there was something wrong."

He drew closer, coming up behind her. "I just can't believe you told them so much of the truth."

"I told them as much as I could. I gave them Dillon's description, said I saw him clearly, and he was the man who shot me. I suppose they may spend a long time looking for someone who looks just like Dillon Waters." She paused. "I still can't believe you rode Lightning out, trying to save me. You're lucky he didn't crash into the side of my truck or something."

"He's a fine horse," Colt replied quietly. "He just needs the right instructor."

"Like you?"

"Like me."

"What did you do about Mav?" she asked.

"I buried him down near the lake, just like you asked," he replied quietly. "I'm sorry you had to lose him the way you did," he said tenderly.

"The inn will be so lonely without him," she said, her voice cracking.

"I'll be there with you . . . if you want me," he offered tentatively. His mouth was suddenly dry.

"Always?" she whispered.

"Always, Red. Everything I said that night in front of Dillon Waters was true."

He pushed her hair aside and kissed her neck. She shivered beneath his lips. "Do you know how much I missed that?" she murmured.

"Yes, as much as I did." He placed another on her shoulder, undoing the tie at the neck of the hospital gown. "You know what we have to do before you can wear that shirt, don't you?"

"What if Nurse Camden comes in?"

"The drill sergeant?"

Lauren laughed softly. "Yes."

"Maybe she'll learn a little love and compassion," he murmured before he undid the last tie of the hospital gown.

Lauren smiled, knowing that with the warmth of Colt's embrace and his promise of always, her nightmare had ended. Forever.

* * * * *

**Silhouette Books
is proud to present
our best authors, their best books...
and the best in your reading pleasure!**

Throughout 1994, look for exciting books
by these top names in contemporary
romance:

DIANA PALMER
Enamored in August

HEATHER GRAHAM POZZESSERE
The Game of Love in August

FERN MICHAELS
Beyond Tomorrow in August

NORA ROBERTS
The Last Honest Woman in September

LINDA LAEL MILLER
Snowflakes on the Sea in September

*When it comes to passion,
we wrote the book.*

BOBQ3

V™ *Silhouette*®

MIRA ™

The brightest star in women's fiction!

This October, reach for the stars and watch all your dreams come true with **MIRA BOOKS.**

HEATHER GRAHAM POZZESSERE
Slow Burn in October
An enthralling tale of murder and passion set against the dark and glittering world of Miami.

SANDRA BROWN
The Devil's Own in October
She made a deal with the devil...but she didn't bargain on losing her heart.

BARBARA BRETTON
Tomorrow & Always in November
Unlikely lovers from very different worlds...they had to cross time to find one another.

PENNY JORDAN
For Better For Worse in December
Three couples, three dreams—can they rekindle the love and passion that first brought them together?

The sky has no limit with **MIRA BOOKS**

Dark secrets, dangerous desire...

Lovers DARK AND DANGEROUS

Three spine-tingling tales from the dark side of love.

This October, enter the world of shadowy romance as Silhouette presents the third in their annual tradition of thrilling love stories and chilling story lines. Written by three of Silhouette's top names:

LINDSAY McKENNA
LEE KARR
RACHEL LEE

Haunting a store near you this October.

The Loop™

Is the future what it's cracked up to be?

This August, find out how C. J. Clarke copes with being on her own in

GETTING IT TOGETHER: CJ
by Wendy Corsi Staub

Her diet was a flop. Her "beautiful" apartment was cramped. Her "glamour" job consisted of fetching coffee. And her love life was less than zero. But what C.J. didn't know was that things were about to get better....

The ups and downs of modern life continue with

GETTING IT RIGHT: JESSICA
by Carla Cassidy in September

GETTING REAL: CHRISTOPHER
by Kathryn Jensen in October

Get smart. Get into "The Loop!"

Only from ▼ *Silhouette*®

where passion lives.

MONTANA Mavericks

Stories that capture living and loving beneath the Big Sky, where legends live on...and the mystery is just beginning.

This October, discover more MONTANA MAVERICKS with

SLEEPING WITH THE ENEMY
by Myrna Temte

Seduced by his kiss, she almost forgot he was her enemy. *Almost.*

And don't miss a minute of the loving as the mystery continues with:

THE ONCE AND FUTURE WIFE
by Laurie Paige (November)
THE RANCHER TAKES A WIFE
by Jackie Merritt (December)
OUTLAW LOVERS
by Pat Warren (January)
and many more!

Wait, there's more! Win a trip to a Montana mountain resort. For details, look for this month's MONTANA MAVERICKS title at your favorite retail outlet.

Only from ▼ *Silhouette*® where passion lives.